"I almost don't ... there," she said.

Tony put his bottles on the table and crossed his arms. He wanted to pull Laura into his arms and hug her, but that would make a bad situation so much worse.

"It's not fair," Laura said.

"No, but you deserve to be out there doing your job. Truth be told, you're one of the best volunteers we've had in a long time. You're smart, you pay attention, and you're brave and dedicated."

She shook her head. "When you say things like that, it makes me feel..."

"What?" he asked gently. He wished he could see inside her thoughts.

"Afraid," she admitted, looking into his eyes. "Afraid of failing, of not knowing what to do and letting someone down at the worst time. Afraid everyone will find out I'm not as brave as I act."

Tony felt his heart pounding. How many times had he had the same thoughts?

Dear Reader,

Thank you for joining me for the second book in the Cape Pursuit Firefighters series. If I had to choose a theme for this book, it would be that a person can help himself or herself by helping others. It's true, isn't it? If you read *In Love with the Firefighter*, in which Nicole and Kevin's love overcame big obstacles, you might recall Nicole's sister Laura. When she visited Cape Pursuit, she was lost and hurting from her brother's death fighting fires. When I wrote her character, I wasn't sure what a happy ending would look like for Laura, but I couldn't stop thinking about her. I'm happy to say Laura Wheeler discovers a way to feel whole again, and she finds it in the last place she would have imagined.

Captain Tony Ruggles was there for Kevin and Nicole in book one, and now he's the chief of the Cape Pursuit Fire Department. When Laura walks in the door of the fire station with a surprising request, he has no idea how strong she is and how much she will capture his heart.

I hope you enjoy this book and come back to Cape Pursuit for the third book releasing in the summer of 2020. As always, I love hearing from readers on my website, amiedenman.com, or via email, author@amiedenman.com, if you feel like saying hello.

Thank you for reading romance!

Amie

HEARTWARMING

The Firefighter's Vow

—

Amie Denman

HARLEQUIN
HEARTWARMING

HARLEQUIN®
HEARTWARMING™

PLEASE RECYCLE
THIS PRODUCT IS RECYCLABLE

Recycling programs
for this product may
not exist in your area.

ISBN-13: 978-1-335-88958-4

The Firefighter's Vow

Copyright © 2020 by Amie Denman

This edition published by arrangement with Harlequin Books S.A.

For questions and comments about the quality of this book, please contact us at CustomerService@Harlequin.com.

Harlequin Enterprises ULC
22 Adelaide St. West, 40th Floor
Toronto, Ontario M5H 4E3, Canada
www.Harlequin.com

Printed in U.S.A.

Amie Denman is the author of twenty contemporary romances full of humor and heart. A devoted traveler whose parents always kept a suitcase packed, she loves reading and writing books you could take on vacation. Amie believes everything is fun, especially wedding cake, show tunes, roller coasters and falling in love.

Books by Amie Denman

Harlequin Heartwarming

Starlight Point Stories

Under the Boardwalk
Carousel Nights
Meet Me on the Midway
Until the Ride Stops
Back to the Lake Breeze Hotel

Cape Pursuit Firefighters

In Love with the Firefighter

Carina Press

Her Lucky Catch

Visit the Author Profile page
at Harlequin.com for more titles.

CHAPTER ONE

THE WIDE WHITE beach of Cape Pursuit, Virginia, stretched as far as Laura Wheeler could see as she shaded her eyes with one hand. The first day of June had already lured summer visitors with hot sun and a just right ocean breeze promised a fresh new start to the season. Hundreds of people dotted the beach under umbrellas or on colorful beach towels, alternately dipping into the salt water and drying off in the heat.

Most people came to Cape Pursuit looking for fun and relaxation, but Laura had come for something else.

She took an assessing glance at the tall freshly-painted lifeguard chairs within her view and, satisfied that everything was under control, turned and walked across the soft sand to the Pursuit of Fun beach shack, which served as both the command center of the public beach and also a snack bar and surfboard rental.

"It's hot," the girl behind the service window said. "And we've already rented out half the surfboards."

"Those are both excellent problems to have," Laura said, smiling.

The girl, Rebecca, laughed. "Plus, I have this terrible view of the beach and ocean and I have to spend all summer here and get paid for it."

Laura nodded sympathetically, her smile becoming lighter. "When you're a famous singer someday, you can pour all this suffering into a song."

Rebecca held a pen as if it were a microphone and belted out a line about killing time at a beach shack in the sun. They both laughed.

"While you're waiting for your record contract and your throngs of adoring fans to come along, I'll set up a few fans of the electric cooling kind," Laura said. She entered the beach hut through a side door and found two big box fans. She plugged them in, then pointed one of them toward Rebecca and the other out the door to draw heat out of the small building. Growing up in a house with no air-conditioning and spending a summer working for a food vendor that traveled to all the county fairs in her home state of Indiana, Laura knew a few tricks for staying cool in the summer heat.

"Do you think I can make it as a singer?" Rebecca asked.

Laura leaned both elbows on the counter next to the teenager. "I think you can do absolutely anything you want to do," she said. "You just have to believe in yourself and never give up."

"That's what my choir teacher said," Rebecca commented. "But it sounds like something printed on one of those motivational wall calendars with pictures of sunrises and stuff."

"I like sunrises and stuff," Laura said as she moved to her small desk and pulled the lifeguard scheduling book toward her. "And teachers are always right when it comes to believing in people."

Laura had spent the past three years trying to believe she was making a difference as a teacher, and she needed all the sunrises and motivational calendars she could get.

"Jason called off again," Rebecca said, her scowl suggesting she didn't like it.

"Did he say why?" Laura asked.

Rebecca snorted. "Something about somebody in his family being sick. Again."

Laura shrugged. "Maybe somebody really is."

"I asked for details last time we worked together, but he didn't have much of a story," Rebecca said. "I wish I was a lifeguard. I'd take his shift. I could use the extra cash."

Laura scrolled through her list of lifeguards who might come in on short notice. Jason had disappointed her twice in the past week without much explanation.

"You should hire somebody else to replace him before summer gets really busy," Rebecca said. "I was here last year and there was zero tolerance for workers who didn't show up."

"Maybe you're right," Laura said. "But I hate to give up on someone too soon." She glanced up at Rebecca and smiled. "You never know who might turn out to be a hidden treasure with an incredible future."

Rebecca shook her head and laughed. "This hidden treasure shows up to work."

"Why don't you become a lifeguard?" Laura asked. "I think you'd be great."

Rebecca sighed. "I just turned fifteen, and even though I told my mom that was the minimum age, she thinks I should wait another year. I tried to get my Aunt Diane to convince her, but she didn't want to upset my mom." Rebecca smiled. "Aunt Diane retired last year, and now she's decided to become a volunteer firefighter here in town. Can you believe that? She starts training next week."

Laura swallowed back the emotion that always bubbled up when she heard, saw or thought about firefighters. Would the memory of her younger brother, Adam, getting on a plane to go west and fight wildfires always hurt so much?

"Do you think my aunt can be a firefighter?" Rebecca searched Laura's face, but Laura quickly put on her schoolteacher smile.

"Of course I do. Anyone can be anything." Laura hoped Rebecca never ran up against a wall she couldn't climb and never lost her enthusiasm.

A family with two young boys approached the window and asked about renting surfboards. While Rebecca helped them, Laura

picked up the phone and called two lifeguards who she knew were anxious for hours
and willing to work extra shifts. She left a
message for the first one, but got through to
the second one and secured a replacement
for the missing Jason.

As she worked through her personnel
problem, she half listened to Rebecca chatting with the young family. They were from
Ohio, and the boys were six and eight. None
of them had ever been on a surfboard or even
gone in the ocean, and Rebecca was giving
them a mini-lesson with lots of hand gestures
and description.

Laura hung up and approached the counter. "Why don't you go out to the beach and
help them get started," she told Rebecca. "I'll
run the counter for a few minutes."

"That would be great," the mother of the
two young boys said, a hopeful smile on her
face. "If you don't mind."

"I'm happy to," Rebecca said. "I love surf-
ing."

Rebecca let the boys choose from a stack
of surfboards and then they bounded across
the beach together. Laura leaned on the counter and watched. She breathed deeply of the

ocean air, closed her eyes and listened to the sounds of the waves and people having fun. A group of young teenagers were laughing and throwing a football back and forth just on the edge of the beach, their feet splashing in the water. A beach volleyball net was set up not far away, and Laura heard the players calling out who had the ball.

A long blast of a whistle forced her eyes open and Laura immediately began scanning the beach area, looking for a sign from the lifeguard who had signaled danger. Although her job was running the business of the rental shack and overseeing summer personnel, Laura knew the basics of lifeguarding. Her experience as a high school teacher and ability to manage teenagers had recommended her for the summer job, and Laura was happy to spend her days on a beach instead of inside a classroom.

But not everything about working on a beach was fun and games. She squinted and saw a lifeguard, Kimberly, waving at someone who was very far out in the water. Were there two people out there? Laura picked up her radio and keyed the microphone. She saw a radio in Kimberly's hand.

"They're pretty far out," Laura said. "Are they okay?"

"Not sure," Kimberly said. "I don't think they hear me, and it looks like they're struggling."

Kimberly was the lead lifeguard on the beach that day and had five summers under her belt working the Cape Pursuit public beach. She'd shared with Laura her excitement about having only one year of college left as she worked toward her degree in marine biology.

Laura felt her pulse in her throat, and she was glad Kimberly had enough experience to sound calm even in the face of a potential rescue.

"Do what you think you should," Laura said. "I'll send you some help."

Laura keyed her radio again, catching the attention of all the lifeguards. "Activate the rescue sequence for a person too far out in the water." When activated, the protocol called for other lifeguards to close their sections of beach, get swimmers out of the water and converge on the area in need of help. Rebecca raced back toward the beach shack as soon as she realized what was going on and stopped, breathlessly, in front of the window.

"Where do you want me?" she asked.

"Stay here and listen to the base radio. I'm going out there to see if I can help, and I'll let you know if you need to call 911."

Laura had been a dedicated runner for over a decade since she had joined her high school cross-country team as a sophomore. She'd been an assistant coach for the team at the high school where she had worked the past three years, and she knew a lot about controlling her breathing and pace.

None of that mattered as she raced across the beach, radio in hand, unsure what she could do but knowing she had to do something. At the very least, she had to make sure that none of the young people under her supervision got themselves killed.

The ocean roared in her ears—or was it her pulsing blood? Close up, the waves seemed much larger than they had from her post in the rental shack.

When Laura reached the edge of the surf, Kimberly was already way out in the water and another lifeguard, Jordan, was making her way out. Laura paused and evaluated the entire scene, trying to make certain the plan, as she knew it, was being followed. No swimmers were in the water, and several lifeguards patrolled long stretches of sand, making certain no one was going in. Satisfied that the entire emergency scene was under control, she returned her attention to Kimberly, who had reached the struggling swimmers.

Kimberly gave Laura the hand signal for help. Laura radioed Rebecca and told her to call 911, then laid the radio on top of her shoes, took a deep breath and plunged in.

A good swimmer but a better runner, Laura stayed on her feet as long as she could. When the waves were over her waist, she threw herself on top of the water and swam freestyle. Every ten strokes or so, she paused and looked forward, making sure she was heading for the small group that included two struggling swimmers and two lifeguards.

The undertow swirled around her legs, but she battled it. Her loose-fitting polo shirt sagged with water and slopped against her side, and her knee-length shorts grew heavy.

She calmed her breathing and stayed in tight control of herself by counting each stroke.

Finally Laura reached Kimberly as she towed a swimmer in. Was the swimmer breathing? Laura searched Kimberly's face for an answer and was reassured with a weak smile.

"They're okay," the lifeguard said. "Just exhausted. Jordan and I got life jackets on them and we're bringing them in."

"I'll help," Laura said. She quickly evaluated both the rescued people—two teenaged boys—and took the arm of the one who needed more help. She saw it in his panicked expression and the way he tried to fight Jordan while also clinging to her.

With one hand on the rescued teen and the other one sweeping broadly as she dug deep with her leg strength to keep moving, Laura helped the two trained lifeguards fight the waves and close the distance to the shore.

Despite the water in her face and her focus on helping the group move, Laura noticed people on the beach. An ambulance. Firefighters in navy blue pants and shirts. As she grew closer, she watched them take off their radios and shoes just as she had done and wade into the water.

Luckily for the firefighters, the five swimmers were in water they could stand up in, and they were walking clumsily the last dozen yards to the firm sand. For the first time since she had entered the water, Laura felt utter exhaustion flood her body. She felt like sinking down on the sand and taking a long nap in the sunshine.

"What do we have?" a voice asked as Laura forced her legs to carry her onto the beach while she supported the teen, whose arms were over her shoulders and Jordan's. She knew that voice.

Laura looked up and saw Tony Ruggles from the Cape Pursuit Fire Department. He was dressed in a navy blue uniform shirt and pants, and his broad shoulders and blond hair looked exactly as she remembered. They hadn't seen each other since the previous summer, but she knew Tony would never forget the impression she had made on him that day.

She was doing a lot better today, despite being drenched, covered in salt and sand, and wearing waterlogged clothes not designed for swimming. Her heart raced as she took in the scene on the beach and handed over the young swimmer to Tony and his partner.

She had taken charge of the first emergency of the summer, acted with strength and courage, and helped save someone. Her body no longer needed the adrenaline surging through her now, and Laura felt like a bubbling pot on a stove, threatening to blow its lid off with pent-up energy.

"Are you okay?" Tony asked. He put both hands on her upper arms and steadied her, looking closely at her face.

Gooseflesh raced over her arms and legs, a physical manifestation of the shock of cold ocean water and excitement. Tony rubbed his hands up and down her arms, and her equilibrium returned. "Laura?" he asked.

Judging from his expression, Laura was afraid he was about to scoop her up and tuck her into the back of the ambulance.

"Never better," she said, meaning it sincerely. She looked past Tony and saw the boys and their rescuers sitting on the sand and smiling together as the other lifeguards and firefighters handed them sports drinks and watched over them.

TONY CAUGHT HIS BREATH. Despite his nearly dozen years of firefighting, his blood still pumped with excitement whenever a call came in. Fires, heart attacks, car accidents, beach rescues. All of them activated his love of coming to the rescue, no matter what. Helping other people live was his reason for living.

Catching his breath was pretty darn hard when he realized the woman on the beach was Laura Wheeler. He had no idea why she was in Cape Pursuit, or at the scene of a beach rescue, but he remembered three things about her from the summer before.

He remembered her eyes filled with pain and vulnerability—a look he'd seen so many times in the fire-and-rescue service. He recalled her hair, soft as silk in his fingers as he'd held it while she vomited up her mistakes from the Cape Pursuit Bar and Grill. And he couldn't forget her dismissal of him… Her dismissal and rejection as if his help had burned her.

Looking at her now, he saw something else. She had the same long dark hair, now streaming with water, but her shoulders were square. Her eyes were the radiant blue he re-

membered, but the expression in them was…
different.

"Everyone seems okay, Chief," his partner, Travis, said, taking Tony's attention
away from Laura and reminding him that
he was the officer in charge, superseding
lifeguards and anyone else when he showed
up on a scene. "Lifeguards did a good job."

Tony grunted. Laura was walking over to
her lifeguards, who were standing together
in a group, animatedly discussing the event.
She touched the shoulders of two of them
and talked with them in a low, calm voice
while Tony and his partner knelt and talked
with the rescued swimmers.

He wondered when Laura had arrived in
town. If she had moved to Cape Pursuit,
he was surprised his cousin Kevin hadn't
mentioned it. Kevin's upcoming wedding to
Laura's sister, Nicole, meant Tony had expected he'd see Laura in July. But why was
she already in town?

"Sure you don't want to go to the hospital?" Travis asked. "Just in case?"

"We're fine," one of the teens said.

"Where are your parents?"

"At the hotel," the other one said, pointing

to one of the many beachfront hotels with balconies overlooking the Atlantic.

"We'll need to talk to them," Tony said. "Which hotel?"

The teen gave him the information and Tony made the call. Within minutes, a middle-aged man and woman were running across the sand, even though both teens were on their feet and waving sheepishly at their approaching parents.

Tony had seen a similar scene more times than he could remember. The relatives showing up at the hospital just after a car accident, concerned adult children skidding into their parents' living rooms as the paramedics were loading up someone with chest pain. He'd seen happy endings like this one, but also gut-wrenching sad ones that both tested and reinforced his resolve to continue being a first responder.

"We're okay," both boys said at the same time. Their parents hugged them, not seeming to care about getting wet or sandy, and Tony gave them space for a minute before he approached. The teens needed a lesson about getting too far out and going beyond the limits of their swimming abilities, and

Tony knew they were probably hearing that message now. He would talk with the parents in a moment and give them their options for further medical care if they felt it was needed.

"Experience is a hard but good teacher," Laura said seriously, her eyes meeting Tony's as she came up to him. A touch of the vulnerability he'd seen the previous summer reappeared for a moment, but then she looked away.

"That's the truth," he said. "I'll write up a full report after I talk to their parents."

"Can I get a copy of that?"

"Uh…sure." Now that the initial shock of seeing her had worn off somewhat, Tony could have a polite conversation. They weren't strangers. "How have you been, Laura?"

Her lips parted for a moment as if she was considering her answer. It was strange, meeting this way after not seeing each other for so long. Tony had wondered about her over the past year.

"I've been fine. How about you?"

"Fine," he said. "I'm just surprised to see you."

"I'm here for the summer," she said. "Working at the Pursuit of Fun beach shack and supervising all the teen workers."

A summer job. Spending time with her sister before she got married. The pieces began to fall into place and Tony felt his shoulders relax.

"Teaching high school is good practice for that, I'd bet," he said.

Laura tilted her head and raised both eyebrows a hair. "You remember I'm a teacher."

"I remember," he said. He didn't elaborate on what else he remembered from the previous summer, as he thought Laura was just as likely to want to forget it. "Are you a lifeguard?"

She shook her head.

"You're not a lifeguard, but you ran into the ocean and tried to save people anyway," he said. Exactly the kind of bystander he and his partners on the fire department didn't love. The kind that often needed to be rescued, too.

"We actually did save them," she said. Her cheeks colored and she crossed her arms.

"You shouldn't put yourself in danger."

"You do it all the time," she said.

"That's different. I'm a trained first responder with a lot of experience."

"You weren't here," Laura said. "And I was. Besides, I'm more capable than you think."

Tony clenched his jaw, not wanting to argue with Laura, knowing he wouldn't win. She was right about being there and being successful, but it could have quickly gone in another direction. Good intentions only went so far and often ended up getting people killed.

"I'll make sure you get a copy of that report," he said.

He grabbed his boots and stomped his feet into them without bothering to tie the laces. He didn't want to think about what could have happened to Laura and how that would have devastated her family, who had already suffered enough.

CHAPTER TWO

LAURA WATCHED THE ambulance depart, envying both Tony and Travis their confidence and bravery. When they rolled up at an emergency, they had no idea what they might face. She could almost forgive Tony for lecturing her about jumping in without training. His censure had been arrogant, irritating…and at least partly true.

Her bare toes were in the sand, and the calming pattern of waves breaking on the beach behind her was as familiar as the sound of her own breathing. But something was stirring her thoughts, not letting her go.

When the fatal news of her brother's loss in a forest fire out west had destroyed her family's peace two years ago, her only thought had been to run away. She hadn't physically run. Until ten days ago, she had continued to live in the home that still had her brother's favorite mug in the kitchen cabinet. Instead, she'd emotionally tried to put distance between herself and that day, and she hadn't succeeded.

Drinking wasn't the answer. Burying herself in American History by attempting to write a historical novel had gone nowhere. Dating a man who loved himself far more than he cared about her… Uh, no. He hadn't been much better than the immature guy she dated after him.

Only one thing had gotten her out her bed on those dark winter mornings, and it was the idea that someone might need her, that someone was suffering more than she was.

"Excellent work," she said to Kimberly and Jordan. "You each get a save on your record." The lifeguards beamed, their wet hair gleaming in the sun. "Go back to the hut and take a break while I get your areas covered and we reopen the beach to swimmers."

Laura followed established protocol, explaining only what was necessary to other beach guests and getting the swimming area back to normal. Laura thought about what could have gone wrong and what she would have done.

If the swimmers hadn't been breathing,

what would she have done? She had her CPR certification from being the assistant coach on the cross-country team. So she probably could have done something. But she could do more, couldn't she? She wanted to do more.

Rebecca's Aunt Diane was becoming a volunteer firefighter. Just like that. Following an idea and a passion. People reinvented their lives all the time and for all sorts of reasons.

She had reasons.

She thought of Tony's words about training and experience. What if she shocked him and herself by becoming a rescuer? The thought was bold and jolted her from her head to her toes. Could she join the fire department? She'd tried volunteering and community service. She'd joined a community group raising money for a food kitchen. She'd spent holidays throughout the school year volunteering instead of sitting at her family's dinner table where someone would always be missing.

She had to admit to herself that her activities had at first been motivated by the need to escape that empty place. And then she'd slowly discovered the truth behind the old saying that helping others was the best way to help herself.

What if she took her volunteer service to a whole new level and became a first responder? As she crossed the beach, she clung to the idea as if it were a valued possession.

Afraid to even say it aloud, she kept the thought to herself throughout the rest of her long shift, but she mulled it over all day. The idea wouldn't let go.

The late afternoon sun had lost some of its intensity when Laura parked her bicycle in front of the Cape Pursuit fire station. She was careful not to block the five massive overhead doors, which were open to reveal shining fire trucks. She had a reason for being there, a solid reason for asking where Tony Ruggles might be so she could get information for her incident report. But she also had a secret fire in her chest.

At the front of the station, a sign with changeable black letters advertised the upcoming volunteer class. Was that the one Diane was taking? Maybe she should call Rebecca's aunt and talk to her?

Those trucks were beautiful. The lights, the chrome, the complicated pumps, the ladders stored along the sides…and the tires. Huge and waist high, the thick black rubber tires looked as if they could plow over any obstacle. The power was intoxicating, and she wanted to learn their secrets. Had her brother felt that way?

"Hello, Laura."

She spun, feeling awkward about her fascination with the trucks. Tony stood, arms crossed, as if she were an intruder in his domain. His dark navy uniform shirt was buttoned neatly, and a silver bar over a chest pocket said Chief Ruggles. Hadn't he been a captain last summer?

"The report," she stammered. "You said I could contact you for information so I can complete my incident report about today's… incident."

He nodded, but his expression didn't change even when she stumbled over her words. She almost wished he would laugh at her and break the tension. Her chest thrummed with excitement, but she wanted to appear calm and deliberate.

"Come into my office," he said.

Laura somehow felt safer in the middle of the wide bay surrounded by the trucks.

They inspired confidence. Tony, with his look of professional neutrality, did not make her feel as if she were a woman on a mission to change her life by changing the world around her.

"Thank you," she said, bravery in her tone. "Lead the way."

Tony had already started to turn toward a long interior wall with several doors down it, but he paused and looked back at her when she spoke. Good. He should know she wasn't intimidated by him.

Tony opened one of the doors in the long wall. Laura entered the cool, dim office with faded color photographs of former chiefs on the walls, a massive steel desk and functional ugly furniture.

"When did you become the chief?" she asked.

"At the end of last summer."

Small talk. It bridged the gap of the past year and built a tiny social foundation between her and Tony, but it was a delay. She needed to tell him her real reason for coming to the fire station.

"Your dad was the chief, wasn't he?"

Tony nodded.

"And you followed in his footsteps."

Tony's forehead wrinkled and Laura recognized irritation in his expression.

"I earned it if that's what you're asking." He tried to smile, but it was nothing like the friendly smile he'd given the kids on the beach, their parents and even his firefighting partner. Her impression of Tony from the previous summer was of a lighthearted but sincere man who would do anything to help someone. But no one likes having their work questioned.

"Of course you earned it," she said, putting enthusiasm behind her words to try to dispel the tension.

Tony's features relaxed. "My dad retired and there was a shift in leadership positions. I was in the right place at the right time. Kevin is a captain now, but your sister probably already told you that."

Before arriving in Cape Pursuit for the summer to live with her sister, Laura talked to Nicole almost every week on the phone and more often via text message and email, but the fire department was not something they typically talked about.

Tony handed Laura a printed copy of the

report from the beach run. "That's an extra. You can take it with you," he said.

Was he dismissing her?

"I wanted to make sure it was available for you since I'm going off duty in about an hour," he added.

Oh. He was being considerate and organized. Of course. He helped people and didn't ask questions. When he'd taken her keys away from her in the parking lot of the Cape Pursuit Bar and Grill and held open the door of his truck, he'd hardly said a word. As she disgraced herself being sick from too many drinks on an empty stomach, he'd held her hair and offered her damp washcloths.

The memory burned her cheeks. If he had seen her over the course of the past year, he would probably have tried to rescue her. The days she'd left her teaching job and sat in the parking lot, head on the steering wheel, fighting tears. The nights she slipped out of the house after her parents were asleep so she could go for long walks without answering questions.

That was why she had come to Cape Pursuit. She was doing so much better than what he probably thought. At least she was try-ing…

"How did you become a firefighter?" she asked, forcing the subject into the open before she chickened out.

Tony cocked his head to the side and drew his eyebrows together.

"I mean, what did you have to do to become qualified?" she asked.

"To be a professional firefighter, you have to take hundreds of hours of training," he said.

"What kind of training?"

Tony's expression softened. "Sit down," he said, indicating one of the much-used chairs in the office. "Please."

Laura sat, but she kept her back straight so she would feel strong and powerful. She needed her strength for what she was about to do.

"I feel like you must have a reason for asking," Tony said, leaning forward with his elbows on his knees. He looked sympathetic, as if he were talking to a lost child. He wasn't much older than she was, and she was not lost. In fact, she was starting to feel quite found. "Is this about your brother?"

"No," Laura said, shaking her head. "It's about me." She took a deep breath and let it out, knowing Tony would be patient enough to wait a moment for her explanation. "I'd like to become a volunteer firefighter."

IT WAS NOT the first time Tony had talked with someone coming into the fire station and asking about joining as either a volunteer or a full-timer. Firefighters tended to attract attention with their high-profile jobs, big trucks and loud sirens. The station, too, was prominently located and took up half a block in Cape Pursuit.

He was glad every time someone came in and asked about joining their ranks because he believed it was the best and most noble profession. Believed in helping others even at the risk of his own life. Believed in his men, his trucks and their training.

He *couldn't* believe Laura Wheeler was sitting in his office asking to sign up. The fact that she was a woman had nothing to do with his shock. Cape Pursuit didn't have any women on the roster, but most local departments did and he'd had female instructors at the fire academy who'd easily dispelled any myth about men being better able to do the job.

No, it wasn't that she was female. It was that she was Laura Wheeler. The woman who had been cast adrift by her firefighter brother's death. He'd asked about her since their meeting last year, indirectly and discreetly. His best friend and cousin Kevin was marrying Laura's sister, so it wasn't far off the mark for Laura to come up in conversation.

Nothing he'd heard would have made him think Laura was a candidate for the fire service, but she was right there looking at him with expectation written in the set of her mouth and intensity in her eyes.

"A volunteer firefighter," she repeated. "Not an astronaut, so you don't need to look so shocked."

"I'm not shocked," Tony said quickly, but he doubted he was very convincing.

"Women can fight fires."

"Yes," he said. "I've known other women in the fire service who could outclimb me on ladders, outdrive me in the trucks and just generally outsmart me."

Laura raised both eyebrows, a look she

had probably perfected with teenagers making up excuses about their homework.

"I just didn't think firefighting…after what happened with…"

"My brother, Adam," Laura said steadily as if she wanted to get it out in the open. "Yes. He died doing this. It was a forest fire, but it was a fire. And yes, I'm sure you think I must be out of my mind to want to do this."

"I don't think you're out of your mind."

"Good," she said. "How can I join the department?"

"We…have an application process. And there's training, of course. Volunteers don't need nearly as much as full-time staff, but there's still a lot you would need to know."

"I know CPR and have first aid training because I was a coach, and I helped save someone just this morning from drowning," she said. "That's a start, isn't it?"

"CPR and first aid training are very relevant," Tony agreed. It was true that teachers and coaches had to be cool under pressure and often put the needs of others first. He respected that, but he hadn't known before today that Laura had any experience or desire that would qualify her to do what he did.

His image of her was as Nicole's sister who didn't always make the best choices.

Tony sat back in his chair and tried to re-imagine Laura as a person capable of wearing thirty pounds of gear, fighting her way through smoke and dousing a fire.

"I'm physically fit," she said as if she could read his thoughts. He was instantly ashamed. The size of a person had little to do with the ability to fight fires. Brains, attitude and training were far greater determiners. "I run."

"That's great," Tony said. "I can see you're very…" He needed to change the subject before he said something stupid. "Have you talked to your sister about this?"

Laura's determined and even slightly defiant expression fell, and Tony knew he'd hit a sore spot. He didn't want to discourage her, but…

He wanted to protect her. That was it. And that was the problem.

"I haven't," she said. "Do you ask every volunteer who comes in here if he's talked to his sister?"

"You're not every volunteer," Tony said, his tone soft.

Laura stood. "Can I have an application, please?"

Tony got up quickly. "It's online. You just fill it out and submit it."

"And when does training start?"

Laura was dead serious. "Next week. We're running a six-week intensive summer training."

"Here at the station?" she asked.

Tony nodded. "And I'm the instructor."

CHAPTER THREE

THE SUNNY MONDAY afternoon was peaceful as Laura and her sister, Nicole, cruised an ocean inlet on their paddleboards. Laura loved the challenge of keeping her balance and getting a good workout, and also spending time with her sister. The steady rhythm of their paddles moving in unison lulled her into believing that finding an even keel was a possibility for her that summer. She'd also decided that balancing over thirty feet of water was a great time to share her firefighting plan with Nicole.

The look her sister gave her did not bode well. Nicole dipped her paddle deep and splashed Laura with ocean water. "That's not funny," Nicole said, resting the edge of her paddle between her feet and balancing on the calm water.

"I didn't mean it as a joke," Laura protested, mirroring her sister's movements. "I'm not kidding."

Nicole held up a finger. "You were supposed to spend the summer with me, have fun, help me with my wedding and take care of Kevin's dog while we go on our honeymoon. That kind of stuff. You weren't supposed to show up in town and give me a heart attack."

"Sorry," Laura said. "I thought you might understand."

"Understand?" Nicole asked, raising her voice. "You thought I would understand that my only sister, my only remaining sibling…" her voice softened and trailed off, and Laura instantly felt like a jerk for not realizing just how much of an impact her decision would have on Nicole.

"This is different," Laura said. "I'm not planning on trying to outrun a forest fire. It's a nice small fire department. I'll get plenty of training—probably more than Adam had before he—"

"No," Nicole said. "I'm learning to live with the fact that Kevin is a firefighter, but I can't deal with potentially losing you, too."

Laura began paddling silently alongside

her sister, watching for marine life under the calm blue water. She'd paddled back home in rivers, but this was one hundred times more beautiful and interesting.

"How did you learn to accept Kevin's job?" Laura asked.

"I had to because I love him. I couldn't make him give up something he loves as the price for being with me."

It was Laura's turn to use her paddle to douse her sister with ocean water.

"Hey," Nicole protested.

"You love me and this is important to me, so what's the difference?"

"You're my sister," Nicole said.

"And?"

Nicole blew out a breath and sat down on her paddleboard. She crossed her legs and laid her paddle across her lap. Laura sat, too, and they let the easy current push them gently around while still staying close to each other.

"Why do you want to do this?" Nicole asked.

Laura trailed a hand in the water. "Because I want to live. And live with myself. I used to believe I could do anything and that anything was possible, but when Adam died, it wrecked my world. You know I was…self-destructive for a while."

"Are you kidding?" Nicole asked with a sympathetic smile. "I thought the third guy in a row you dated who had a seedy past and a sketchy future was an indication of your excellent judgment."

"There were only two. And they weren't all that bad. At least I didn't think so at the time."

Nicole nodded. "Of course, I'm getting some of this bias from Mom and Dad who thought you'd quit your teaching job and take off on a motorcycle at any moment. They were worried about you."

Laura forced a laugh, but her sister's words hit home. Her parents, hardworking Midwesterners, considered quitting a nice steady job one of the worst things a person could do. She remembered how scandalized they'd been when Nicole quit her job at the furniture factory a year ago and moved to Cape Pursuit to work in a fledgling art gallery. They'd accepted her decision when the move turned out to be a good one, but Laura wasn't sure they'd see it the same way with her. She was their youngest child now, and she knew they considered her fragile. She would need to prove her strength to them.

"I don't care for motorcycles," Laura said. "There's no good place to put your purse."

"Seriously," Nicole said. "Why firefighting? Do you think it's what Adam would want you to do? Is that why?"

Laura shook her head. "It's what I want to do. Over the past year, the only times I felt better about myself were the times I was helping someone else. I didn't feel the anguish or helplessness I felt after Adam's death while I was being useful volunteering and organizing fundraisers."

"So you could volunteer at all kinds of things," Nicole said, excitement in her voice as she latched onto an idea. "We have a library and a summer reading program in Cape Pursuit. You could work at the soup kitchen. You could organize a sock drive for the homeless. Be a blood donor. You could do fifteen dozen things other than be a firefighter."

"I want to challenge myself," Laura said. "I helped save some people during a beach rescue last week. It was exhilarating and it made me feel like I could get out of my own way for the first time in a long time. I want to help people when they need it the most."

She thought of Tony coming through for her at a dark moment a year before. She had almost gotten behind the wheel of her sister's car after too many drinks to count—her crappiest day in a year full of crappy days. He had rescued her, but she pushed that thought aside whenever it surfaced. Tony wasn't the person who could save her.

The only person who could save her was herself.

She saw Nicole swipe a tear away. She didn't want to argue and open a wound that would never be fully healed. They were sisters. They needed and loved each other.

"Anyway," Laura said as she heaved a big sigh and stood on her board, taking a moment to regain her balance. "I don't even know if they'll accept me into the training program. I'm only here for the summer, and they probably have plenty of people with better qualifications than I have."

Nicole stood on her board and spread her feet carefully, tilting the board side to side and using her paddle as a balance bar until she gained control.

"I don't think anyone coming into the fire service has better qualifications than you do," Nicole said. "You're a superstar teacher, your patience is battle-tested from putting up with teenagers and I think you're braver than you know."

"Really?" Laura said hopefully. Did her sister really believe in her?

"Of course," Nicole said. "You're here helping me with my wedding, and you're crazy enough to live in the same house with me as I panic about all the details. Maids of honor should probably get special presidential medals of valor."

"I thought you were being serious about me being a good candidate," Laura protested, laughing.

"I believe you can do anything you want to," Nicole said. "But I don't want you doing this."

The sisters paddled toward the dock where Kevin sat on the tailgate of his pickup truck, his legs dangling. As soon as they reached the dock, he jumped down from the truck and offered them both a hand.

Nicole stepped onto the dock first, her

paddle in one hand, and then Kevin steadied Laura as she did the same.

"Did you see anything interesting?" he asked. "Stingrays or jellyfish?"

"A shark followed us, but I fought him off with my paddle," Nicole said.

Kevin clutched both her arms. "Really?" he said, his voice full of alarm.

Nicole laughed. "No."

Kevin blew out a sigh of relief.

"Laura fought him off," Nicole said.

Her fiancé shook his head. "Not funny—not that I doubt you, Laura."

He helped haul the paddleboards up to his truck, then lifted them in and secured them with a bungee cord.

"Did you know Laura wants to be a volunteer firefighter?" Nicole demanded as the three of them squeezed into the cab of the truck, Nicole taking the middle seat.

Laura leaned forward so she could see Kevin's face when he answered. His expression was neutral and cautious.

"Tony mentioned that."

"And you didn't tell me?"

"I thought Laura would tell you," Kevin said.

Nicole scoffed. "Coward."

Laura leaned back, happy her sister had someone else to vent her frustration on, even though she knew she hadn't heard the last of it.

Why firefighting? Her sister's question stuck with her. Why the fire service and not one of the dozens of other volunteer possibilities? Nicole's assertion that it was an homage to their brother made Laura pause. Was that her reason?

She had to admit that was part of it. The ultimate way to handle her grief and guilt over Adam was to face it directly, not to run from it as she had been. If she hadn't shown him the campus flyer asking for volunteers, he might never have known about the summer job. He might be alive right now.

She swallowed and took a deep breath, trying to remember to focus on the present and the future—the only things she could do anything about. Being in Cape Pursuit took her away from her parents, but she could be with Nicole. And the blue water, sunshine and vacation vibe of the town had warmed and welcomed her. She could see why Nicole had fallen in love in more ways than one.

Laura watched the downtown shops blur

past as Kevin drove them to her sister's house. Cape Pursuit was where she wanted to be, and squeezing every ounce of bravery she possessed out of her was the way to start over and be whole again.

She'd been planning to tell Nicole she wanted to quit her teaching job, but given her sister's reaction to her plans to join the fire department, Laura decided to save that additional bombshell for another day. Her family wouldn't understand, and she doubted she could explain it in a coherent way because she hardly understood it herself.

"You're not going to try to talk her out of it?" Nicole asked, tapping her fingers on Kevin's knee as he drove. "I thought you had to be on my side since we're getting married."

"Maybe I could think of some arguments if you give me some time," he said. "But I have to go to a class in Virginia Beach as soon as I drop you off. Tony's meeting me at your house so we can get on the road and not be late."

Nicole dropped the subject as they turned onto her street, and Laura saw Tony's truck parked in front of Nicole's house. It brought back the memory of the previous summer when Tony had driven her in that truck back to the house and stayed with her for hours, even when she hadn't deserved his kindness.

She wasn't that person anymore, and she needed to prove that to everyone…starting with herself.

TONY WAITED NEXT to his truck while Kevin carried the paddleboards into the garage and Nicole followed him to help secure them on brackets along the wall. The garage was just large enough for Nicole's small red car, and Tony noticed that Laura was keeping her vehicle tucked alongside the driveway.

"Did you have fun?" Tony asked, hoping to fill up their few minutes together in the driveway with neutral conversation. He was afraid of the negative impression he'd given Laura when she approached him about joining the fire department. He didn't want her to think he didn't believe she could do it, and she'd have other obstacles to face.

"We did," she said. "I love being on the water."

"It's different here than it is back in Indiana, though, isn't it?" he asked. He tried to picture rivers and freshwater streams, but he'd hardly traveled outside of Virginia and the Atlantic coast region.

"Very. At home, all the beautiful scenery is above the water, but here it's above and below the surface."

Below the surface. Tony wondered what was beneath the surface of Laura Wheeler.

"I hope you'll get to enjoy it a lot this summer," he said.

"I downloaded the application," she said. "For the volunteer department."

"About that," he began. It had occurred to him that her residency in Virginia was temporary and that she probably didn't even have a Virginia driver's license. Not being a resident would prevent her from getting certified as a volunteer firefighter in the state.

"I didn't look at it yet," Laura said. I planned to do it later today since it's my day off—I asked for Mondays because that's the day the gallery is closed."

"That's great," Tony said.

"Were you about to tell me something?" Laura asked. "You don't have to reveal any secrets if you don't want to," she added quickly.

"Nothing special. It asks for your contact information, relevant background and experience, special skills you have and why you want to be a firefighter."

"Okay." Laura nodded.

Tony swallowed and looked toward the garage. He wished Kevin would hurry up and finish stowing the paddleboards so they could get on the road to the evening class they were both taking to advance their careers.

"There's no test to get started, right?" she asked.

"No. Just a criminal background check, standard procedure for anyone wanting to join. And you need a valid Virginia driver's license."

Laura bit her lip and looked nervous, and Tony was afraid he'd destroyed her dream. He didn't want to see Laura put her life in danger in the line of duty, but he also didn't want to wreck her hopes with a technicality. Even though that technicality might be the easy way out for him.

"I'm going to the license bureau after work tomorrow to transfer my Indiana license to a Virginia one. I hope that won't slow down the process for my application."

"Transfer? Does that mean you're planning to…stay in Cape Pursuit?"

"I drive vehicles for my job supervising the beach guards and surf shack, and for insurance purposes it makes it a lot easier for them if I have a Virginia license," she said.

Tony noticed that she hadn't answered his question, and there was no polite way for him to pry further.

He'd noticed that Laura was not afraid to ask tough questions, which didn't quite fit with the picture he'd formed last summer. He wished he knew her better, but there was no way he could say that, either. Not if she planned to join the department and be under his supervision as a trainee and member. A personal interest or relationship was definitely out of the question, especially since he was the youngest fire chief in the area. He always felt he had to be careful to act twice as professionally as the other chiefs.

He would have to be content with the information she offered. If she offered it.

"You'll need a few character references," he said. "But I'm sure that won't be a problem for you. You can put down people you worked with in Indiana. Or maybe Kevin."

She pulled off her ball cap and ran a hand through her long dark hair. "So I hear you're in the wedding party, too," she said, nodding toward the garage where Kevin was giving Nicole a long goodbye kiss.

"Groomsman," Tony said after a split second in which he wrapped his head around the change of subject. "And you're the maid of honor."

It wasn't a question. He already knew all the members of the small wedding party. He'd been involved in the planning because the reception following the beach wedding was in the fire station. They didn't rent out the station as a party venue, but Tony remembered a few firefighters' wedding receptions and parties in the past. And the station hosted an elaborate Christmas party every year for members and their families. With the trucks outside and enough decorations, the building could be pretty festive.

Laura nodded. "I still need a dress. Nicole and I decided to wait until I got here so we could go shopping together."

"I haven't been given my instructions

since the wedding is still six weeks away, so I don't know what I'm wearing."

"I do," Laura said. "I helped Nicole pick it out."

"Tell me it's not a white tuxedo. The glare on the beach would blind everyone and they wouldn't be able to tell the bride from the groomsmen," Tony said. "Plus, I'd feel stupid in a white tuxedo."

He was glad to have something to talk about with Laura. Every exchange they had might bring him closer to understanding what motivated her and how he could decide if letting her join his department was the best way of helping her.

Not that she'd asked him to help her.

Laura laughed. "Relax. You're wearing navy blue suits. Rented, matching, and you don't even have to pick out your own ties."

Tony swiped a hand across his brow. "Huge relief," he said, grinning.

He thought ahead and realized that the new training class would finish at the same time as the wedding. When Nicole walked down the aisle and married Kevin, Laura could be ready to be a volunteer member of the Cape Pursuit Fire Department. But would she officially join the department? It didn't cost him anything to let her join the class since he was running it anyway and the prospective volunteers would use borrowed equipment. Still, it was unusual to train a volunteer who appeared to have no plans to stick around. He wanted to ask how long she planned to stay, but then he remembered her response to his question about whether she'd consulted her sister. She would probably ask him if he asked all potential volunteers how long they planned to stay in the area.

"Are you going back to Indiana after the wedding?" he asked instead, hoping Laura would consider his question a natural offshoot of their conversation instead of a pointed question about her dedication.

"I'm in no hurry," she said and didn't elaborate further.

He wondered if Laura had anyone special back home. She was physically beautiful, although in a different way from her sister, and Tony doubted that she had escaped the notice of the opposite sex. What impact would an attractive young woman have on his department? He immediately felt a streak of shame at the thought. He hadn't considered the physical appearance of any of the other volunteers. But Laura was different. She was practically family now that her sister was marrying his cousin. He should look after her if he could.

"Ready?" Kevin asked as he strode toward them. Tony turned away from Laura and began to follow his cousin, but Laura put a light hand on his arm. It was a friendly gesture, but her soft touch reminded him that he should keep his distance.

"What's the training you're going to?" she asked.

"Incident command training. We're taking an advanced course for officers in the fire service. It's good if you want to move up the ranks, and it's also good for continual improvement."

"Haven't you moved up as far as you can get already?" Laura asked.

"Being the chief is a huge responsibility, and there's always something to learn."

Tony had no intention of being one of those leaders who rests on his accomplishments. Becoming the chief at the age of only thirty meant he had a lifetime of leadership ahead of him. He wouldn't let down his department or tarnish his father's legacy.

Laura smiled. "Then I guess I'll be in good hands when the training starts next week."

"I hope so," Tony said. Something about having Laura in his class and potentially under his command brought home all the heavy responsibility of being a leader in a very dangerous job.

CHAPTER FOUR

EVEN THOUGH SHE knew it was stupid, Laura changed her outfit three times before heading to the fire station for the first night of training. She'd obsessed over every detail in the online application and fussed with her exact word choice in the short essay about why she wanted to be a firefighter. She hadn't wanted to appear too eager or they'd think she was a risky candidate with a thirst for danger. But she hadn't wanted to seem too matter-of-fact either, because they might think she was lukewarm about public service.

Laura had asked her summer worker Rebecca for her Aunt Diane's phone number, and the two of them had exchanged messages and even met for coffee. It would be a comfort walking into the class already knowing someone, and they had discussed their answers on their applications. Her sister, Nicole, had drawn the line at helping Laura get on the department. She wasn't going to stop her, but she certainly wasn't going to proofread her work and advise her on what to wear.

Which was why Laura rejected the first pair of jeans with a college T-shirt. And the next pair of chinos with a button-down blouse. She finally settled on jeans with a navy blue elbow-length T-shirt. Not too casual, definitely not dressy or frilly. What if they had to climb a ladder or pull hoses off a truck in an icebreaker sort of event?

She paired practical sneakers with her outfit and grabbed a shoulder bag in case there were books. She hoped for bookwork. If there was something she could read up on, she'd be in her element. A quiz or essay? Golden.

Despite her enthusiasm, her confidence would be a whole lot stronger if she knew what to expect. She drove her car—a blue hatchback with all-wheel drive that suited the winter conditions in Indiana—instead of riding her bike because it would be dark when she returned to her sister's place. Nicole was spending a lot of time with Kevin in anticipation of their wedding in six weeks, and Laura was in the lucky position of having a fully furnished house all to herself most of the time.

She parked on a side street near the station and noticed another car doing the same thing. She wished she had arranged to ride with Diane, but she knew she had to step outside her comfort zone, anyway. Two men got out of the car and walked in the same direction she was. After crossing one street and staying together, Laura smiled at the men.

"Are you going to the fire station?" she asked.

They nodded.

"Me, too," she said. She took a breath and made herself say it out loud, testing the words that represented such a bold move for her. "I'm signing up to be a volunteer firefighter."

There was a slight hesitation, and then the younger man stuck out his hand. "Richard," he said. "I'm starting the volunteer class tonight, too. And this is my brother, Oliver."

"Ollie," the other man said.

"I'm Laura." As she shook hands with both men and they started walking together toward the station, Laura relaxed. They were both in their twenties like her, and maybe they were also nervous about what they were about to do.

"Have you ever done anything like this before?" Ollie asked.

"Not exactly," Laura said. "I did some coaching so I know CPR and basic first aid. I'm not a great cook, so I did have to put out a kitchen fire once."

"Really?" Richard asked.

"Don't get your hopes up," Laura said, laughing. "It was mostly a boil-over that I knocked down by putting the lid on. I have a habit of reading while I'm cooking, and it doesn't always turn out well."

As they approached the open doors of the station, Laura saw others already gathering. How many people were here for the class? She nodded politely at them, wondering if they were trainees or perhaps just visiting friends or relatives at the station.

"Hey, Laura," Diane said. Her short brown hair with a few grays sprinkled in curled over her ears and the rims of her glasses, and she wore a pink T-shirt, jeans and an unzipped Cape Pursuit sweatshirt. "I may be the oldest person in the class," she said, lowering her voice and looking around at the people standing nervously in the station. "But I'm hoping wisdom will make up for it."

Laura was about to assure her that wisdom trumped a lot of things, youth included, but a door opened along a side wall and Tony stepped out. "In here," he said. "Welcome to the first night of firefighter training."

He held open the door and nodded at each of the new recruits. "Sign-in sheet on the table and name tags," Tony said. "You only have to wear name tags the first night, and then I'm sure we'll all get to know each other without them."

Laura was the last one through the door. She glanced at the line ahead of her. There were a total of eight people in the class. Not too many names to remember, but also a small group, making it impossible to blend in.

"Sit anywhere," Tony said. He moved to a table set up at the front of the room. Laura guessed the department used the room for regular meetings and training, because there were three rows of eight chairs each. As the last person to move toward the seats, she found her options were limited. In typical fashion, the six men in the class had spread out in rows two and three, leaving seats in between them. Laura couldn't take any of the buffer seats without looking incredibly awkward.

Diane had taken a seat at the end of the first row farthest from Tony, but Laura parked herself squarely in the front row in front of him.

The seats creaked and Laura crossed and uncrossed her legs, trying to settle into the wooden folding chair. She heard whispered conversations behind her and she caught Diane's eye and smiled at her. Tony shuffled papers next to a set of spiral-bound books on the table in front of her. She knew they weren't waiting for any more class members because hers had been the last name unchecked on the sheet by the door and she'd taken the last name tag and written LAURA in neat capital letters.

Tony cleared his throat. "I think we can get started. I'm Chief Tony Ruggles, and I'll be your instructor for the next six weeks. A little bit about me—I've been on the department for twelve years, since I was eighteen and could officially join, but I've been hanging around since I was old enough to walk. My dad was the chief, and I have several cousins and other relatives on this department or in the fire service. I got my instructor's certificate two years ago, and you are my third class of volunteers."

He paused and turned down the volume on his radio, which he placed on the desk.

"We'll be together quite a lot in the next six weeks and beyond, so I'd like to get a sense of what brought you here tonight and what you hope to get out of this class. We appreciate your willingness to serve, and I'm not going to sugarcoat anything. Our volunteers get in the thick of it right alongside the full-time guys. I can't promise you'll never be in danger, but I can promise I'll do everything I can to prepare you to handle it."

He let his words soak in for a few seconds. "Let's go around the room, have you tell us your names and a little about yourselves and why you've decided to join the department. We can start in the back," he said, vaguely gesturing toward the brothers two rows behind Laura.

"I'm Richard," one of the men Laura had met before class said. "I work at the surfboard factory outside town, and they need some of us to get some fire training because we work with a lot of flammable materials. Insurance company dictating it, you know. So I figured I'd learn something about putting out fires to help me get ahead at work, and I wouldn't mind volunteering and helping out my hometown, too."

"Oliver," the next man said. "My brother talked me into coming," he said, jerking a thumb at Richard, "but I like the idea of doing something more interesting than teaching welding at the vocational school. I guess you could say I play with fire at work, and this is the opposite."

Laura liked both brothers, and they had solid reasons for being there. She focused on listening to her new classmates while also thinking of what she was going to say. She couldn't say, *I'm Laura and I'm here because my brother was killed fighting fires and I think this is the best way for me to heal my own soul while helping others.*

Tony pointed to the next man in the back row. "Skip," he said. "My uncle is a firefighter over in Virginia Beach, and he let me hang out with them and even ride along on a few calls. I just graduated from high school, and I want to be a firefighter like my uncle. I'm getting my feet wet as a volunteer, but I'm hoping I don't stop there."

Tony smiled at the guy. "Always room in the fire service for another good man. Or woman," he added, nodding at Laura and Diane. Laura felt heat radiate up her neck at being singled out and Diane was frowning when Laura glanced over at her.

"Sorry," Tony said. "I didn't say that to be a jerk. I really mean it. There are some amazing women in the fire service."

"Thank you," Diane said with a congenial smile, and Laura admired her instantly for being nonplussed in an embarrassing situation. Maybe she was right about wisdom.

"I'm Brock," a man in the second row said, cutting through the tension. "I officially retired from the city last year, and I'm driving for the senior center, delivering meals now. I think I'd be more useful if I learned how to handle an emergency, and I was glad to see there wasn't a maximum age for volunteers when I filled out the application."

"Me, too," Diane said. Brock had to be in his fifties, and Diane had already told Laura she was forty-eight, so Laura could understand Diane's relief at not being the oldest person in the class.

"I might as well go next since I opened my big mouth. I'm Diane, my house is a quiet empty nest and I've always wanted to drive a fire truck."

"Can't argue with that," Tony said, his eyes crinkling at the corners as he pointed out the last two men in the middle row.

"Allen," a dark-haired, broad-shouldered man with a thin smile said. "I can drive a truck and I've never backed off from a challenge. I'm not afraid of anything, so I think I'm the kind of guy you can use."

Tony kept a polite expression, but Laura noticed the smile had disappeared from his eyes. "I'll be the first to admit that I've been afraid a few times. Justifiably afraid. But knowing what to do in those situations is the best way to keep yourself and your partners alive, and that's what you're going to learn in this class."

Laura heard Allen's chair creak, and she

wondered how he'd received the subtle put-down from Tony.

"I know you, Marshall, but I don't know if anyone else does," Tony said, pointing to the only person left aside from Laura.

"I'm Marshall, and I've been on the police department here for five years. Sometimes we get called to the same situations the fire department does, and I'd like to be more knowledgeable and more helpful in those situations. That's why I'm here."

"And we appreciate it," Tony said. "In a small town like this, you'd be surprised by how much crossover there is between the police and fire departments. In fact," he said, pointing to Laura, "we work with the beach rescue also, where our last class member comes from."

Was Tony trying to help her by giving her a cue or a suggestion of what to say? She couldn't claim he was treating her differently than the other volunteers, but something about this half introduction made it seem as if he were trying to encourage her. Was he?

"I guess it's my turn," she said, smiling and turning in her seat to face her seven classmates. "I'm Laura, and I am working on the public beach this summer. I'm not a lifeguard, but I helped rescue someone last week and it was part of what inspired me to be here tonight."

Part, but not all, and maybe as time passed and she knew her classmates better, she would eventually tell them. But not tonight.

"You did a great job," Tony said, and Laura felt the uncomfortable attention of everyone in the room. Was this how Tony was going to act? Drawing attention to her, even in a positive way? It wasn't what she wanted, but it would be hard to tell him to knock it off when he was being nice. She didn't want to come off as defensive.

The door to the meeting room opened and a young firefighter dressed in uniform came in. He moved with confidence to the front of the room and stood next to Tony.

"This is Gavin Kennedy," Tony said, introducing the firefighter. "He'll be helping me with this class. He's only been out of the academy two years, so he remembers what it's like to be in your shoes."

Gavin smiled politely as Tony picked up

the stack of books and handed them to his helper. "Pass these out."

"Sorry I missed the introductions," Gavin said. As he handed a book to each class member, he read their name tags and said their names aloud. "I'm bad with names, so I'm going to need to practice." When he got to Laura, he paused and said, "Hey, you're Nicole's sister. Kevin told me you were coming."

Laura smiled, wondering how much Kevin had said about her. Did the other men on the department know about her brother's death?

"Let's take a quick look at your books," Tony said. "These will also serve as an overview of the class. There are twelve chapters, and we'll cover one most nights, but you'll have to read a lot on your own. We'll meet here for three hours each of the next Tuesday and Thursday nights, and you'll also be expected to be here for truck inspections, meetings and trainings on Sunday mornings."

Laura ran a finger down the table of contents. Fire behavior. Fire suppression. Emergency scenes. Hazardous materials. As a teacher, she was confident in her ability to read, break down information and memorize what was necessary. The book work would be the easy part. When it came to putting on heavy gear and testing her strength and will against a real fire, she would have to dig deep.

"Chapter one," Tony said. "Becoming a firefighter." He looked up and smiled. "I knew I was going to be a firefighter all my life, but that didn't mean I knew what I was doing. When I screwed up as a rookie, nobody cared that I was the chief's son. They were letting me know about my shortcomings."

"Uh-oh," Oliver said, and he was greeted by nervous laughter.

"Don't worry," Tony said. "I'll share my wisdom. For example, don't put on your seat belt and then try to pull on your turnout coat and fasten it. You might be successful getting the coat on while you're on the way to a fire, but you'll just about kill yourself trying to get out of the truck."

Laura smiled, imagining the scene. She hardly took her eyes off Tony as he stood just four feet in front of her, holding the class's attention. Gavin jumped in with a detail or story a few times, but Tony held the floor as he walked the class through the book and gave them an understanding of what the next six weeks would entail. She knew many instructors back home, but none of them had commanded her interest and respect as Tony did. He was strong, compassionate and more attractive than she wanted to admit to herself. Finally, he closed his book—dog-eared and with sticky notes spilling over the top like a bad hair day—and glanced at the wall clock, which was fashioned to look like a fire truck. Its hands were miniature fire hoses, telling them almost half the class had gone by. She was amazed, but it also worried her. With only twelve class nights to learn everything she needed to know, it already seemed to be going too fast.

"Break time," Tony said. "Feel free to use the restroom and get a soda from the pop machine. Say hello to the guys working tonight and check out the trucks."

TONY WENT DIRECTLY to his office, closed his door and sat behind his desk, enjoying the silence for a moment. He had gladly signed up for the series of courses that would qualify him as an instructor because he'd been inspired by a great teacher himself. He knew the fire service needed the right people training the next generation of firefighters.

He just wished he could fast-forward through the classroom lectures and get to the hands-on stuff that would really make the difference between life and death. As he soaked in a few minutes of solitude, he kept an ear tuned to the station beyond his door. He heard a truck door shut. A chirp of a siren. Radio traffic that made up the background music of his life. Conversations. Laughter.

Gavin's booming laugh shot through him. Had he been flirting with Laura, or had it been Tony's imagination? He tried to shut it out, but he imagined Gavin out there, regaling Laura with stories of his own heroism and trying to impress her. As a new member of the department, Gavin had a tendency to take risks to prove himself. He had tried to rush into a house fire without waiting for his partner once, and he'd shown up at an accident scene while off duty and tried to help despite the fact that there were on-duty guys there with protective gear.

His offenses were the result of trying too

hard, too fast, not a lack of integrity or training. Admirable, but dangerous. Young guys
like Gavin were the reason older guys with
experience were in charge. One of the reasons Tony had selected Gavin to help train
the new recruits was to remind him he was
relatively new himself and didn't know everything. But Tony was beginning to wonder if he'd made a mistake. Would Gavin's
assistance have the opposite effect on the
young hotshot?

He got up and opened his door.

"Kennedy," he barked into the station
where Gavin was holding open the door of
the firetruck and laughing with whomever
was inside. Tony imagined it was Laura, and
the thought of Gavin flirting with her irritated him right under the collar of his uniform shirt.

Gavin turned to face him and the person
in the truck slid out. It wasn't Laura. It was
Diane, the older lady in the class. Gavin offered her a hand as she stepped down from
the pumper.

"Need to see me, sir?"

Tony nodded and gestured into his office.
When Gavin entered and took a seat, his face

all innocent friendliness, Tony took a moment and closed his office door before sitting down himself.

"Do you know why I chose you to help me teach this class?" he asked.

Gavin shrugged, his expression unwavering. "Low seniority?"

"I have plenty of seniority and I'm here," Tony said.

"But you're the instructor. I'm the guy who hands out books and sets up obstacle courses and ladders. Not that I mind. Gotta pay my dues."

Tony blew out a breath and leaned back in his chair.

"Everyone seems like they have a good reason for being here," Gavin continued. "I missed the first part, but then I was talking with the two brothers and that older guy while we looked over the trucks. They seem like they'll be good volunteers."

Tony noticed that Gavin didn't say anything about Laura, and it occurred to him that perhaps he was the one putting too much thought into her presence, not Gavin. He'd been about to lecture Gavin about singling out any of the class members or being too friendly with them, but he checked his words. Just because he found Laura distracting didn't mean any of the other men on the department would feel the same way. He needed to keep his awareness of her carefully controlled, just like a small flame he didn't dare let turn into a wall of fire.

"I wanted to say thank you for helping out," Tony said. "I think you're perfect for the job."

Gavin grinned. "That's what you're paying me for. Can I go out and show them around the rest of the station now?"

Tony nodded and noted the time. He'd wait at least ten minutes before he reconvened the class. He sorted through a stack of fire reports he'd printed from the previous week. He liked seeing things on paper, so he usually printed the reports filed by the firefighters and paramedics, searching the text to make certain his men had followed protocol, achieved the fastest response time possible and worked for the best resolution of every emergency. He took a pen and flagged a few things he wanted to ask about, runs that he hadn't been on. Why had the ambulance spent so much time on scene when called to a home for a seizure patient? What had prompted the officer in charge to call for a medical helicopter on standby when they responded to a kitchen fire at a vacation home on the north side of town?

Tony slept well because he'd grown up with a dad who was a fire chief. When he'd confessed to his father that worrying about the station kept him up at night, his dad sat him down and told him in his blunt way that he'd be no damn good to anyone if he stayed awake all night worrying about what could happen and then was too tired when it did happen.

Not sympathetic, but undeniably true.

Tony finished his notes and left them on his desk so he could focus on the training instead of agonizing over the dangers his new volunteers could face under his command and responsibility.

Gavin had everyone back in the training room and seated when Tony entered. Instead of taking up a position behind the desk, Tony picked a chair at the end of the middle row and sat down with his students.

"I'm glad to see you all came back," he

said. "And I didn't bore you to tears or scare you away."

A few of the guys laughed politely, and Laura got up and turned her chair so she could face him. She smiled and waited with her book open in her lap and her pen poised over it. Tony wondered if Laura's students looked at her with anticipation as if she had the secrets of the universe at her command. That was what her expression seemed to convey.

If Laura believed he knew everything about being a successful firefighter, he couldn't disappoint her. He owed her and everyone else in the class his very best instruction. It could mean the difference between life and death.

CHAPTER FIVE

LAURA SPREAD HER mat in a spot between her sister, Nicole, and their friend Jane. Jane was Nicole's friend and employer, and Laura had been invited warmly into the friendship the previous summer. Going to the gym with them took Laura straight out of her comfort zone.

"This is not my usual thing," Laura said as she watched the other women confidently choose weights from the racks and exercise bands from a hanging peg. "Can't we just go run ten miles?"

"No," Nicole said. "You know I can barely run around the block. You got all the running talent in the family. Or insanity. Hard to tell."

"I'd probably barf after two miles," Jane said. "And I'm tired of smelling like barf all the time already. No one tells you that about having a baby. They're cute, but the smell of old barf on your collar is not even a little adorable."

"You'll be fine," Nicole told her sister. "Just don't try to prove anything, go with a lighter weight if you need to, and feign a broken leg if it gets too tough. We'll back you up by looking very sympathetic and covering you with a sweaty towel."

"Thanks."

The instructor turned on the music and everyone stopped talking. Nicole and Jane looked like they could teach the cardio sculpt class. They had coordinating tights and tops. They moved a little with the music as if they had no trepidation about what came next.

"Just follow along," Nicole said, bobbing her head with the beat and smiling. "You're allowed to not be good at something."

"I've been proving that theory for years," Laura said, and Nicole shook her head and laughed.

"Start with two weights," the instructor called out. "We'll do fifteen reps across the body, fifteen triceps and fifteen side raises."

The reps seemed easy at first, and Laura made a quick switch for heavier weights from the stack at her feet. After ten counts, the weights got even heavier, and by fifteen she regretted her bold move.

"You're not going to be able to lift your arms to wash your hair tomorrow," Nicole whispered between sets. "Pick a lighter weight or you'll have to try dry shampoo. You'd hate it with all your thick hair."

Laura tried to think about how strong she was going to be as she kept going through the next murderous set of exercises. She would owe herself chips and salsa while studying later with her new friend Diane.

"Running is easier," Laura commented after the group had completed three sets of the arm exercises and the instructor told them to grab a quick drink before they moved on to legs.

"But running does nothing for your arms. I have to look good in a wedding dress soon, and you made me get the sleeveless one," Nicole said.

"It's a summer beach wedding. Sleeveless was the only choice," Laura said. "You'll be gorgeous."

"Are you getting ready for a test at the fire station?" Jane asked. "Do you have to carry a fifty-pound bag of kitty litter up a ladder and across a rooftop or something to get on the department?"

"Actually it's a fifty-pound bar of chocolate. If you get it up a ladder, through a burning building and down a fire escape before it melts, you get to eat it. Built-in motivation," Laura said.

Nicole cocked her head and looked serious. "I wonder if Kevin had to do that."

Jane laughed. "Charlie is terrible at resisting temptation of any kind, so he'd probably eat half the chocolate before the test."

"Just kidding," Laura said. "It's a fifty-foot reel of hose, which weighs a lot more than you'd think. I picked one up at our first night of training last night."

"Then you're in the right place," Jane said.

"Unless you come to your senses and start volunteering at the library instead," Nicole added.

"Squats," the instructor said. "You'll want a heavier weight for this one."

"Of course I will," Laura said.

Nicole and Jane laughed, and Laura threw herself into mentally counting along with the instructor.

"You'll be the strongest one in the new

class of volunteers," Jane said as they changed their shoes in the locker room and toweled off sweat. "That fifty-pound hose won't know what hit it."

"I hope so," Laura said. "I've been running for so long, I forgot I had other muscles."

"Let's get smoothies," Nicole suggested. "The gym has a little patio out back where you can show up sweaty and no one cares."

Laura stuffed her shoes and yoga mat into her gym bag and followed the other women to the promised land of sunshine and smoothies. Despite the fact that she was going to be all kinds of sore the next day, she felt light and happy being with people who were also starting a new phase of their lives. Jane had a baby with her new husband, firefighter Charlie Zimmerman, and Nicole was about to marry Kevin.

Laura didn't have a man or a baby, but she had homework. Reading her fire service training books late into the night had made her even more excited about the upcoming second night of class.

"How do you like your job on the beach?" Jane asked.

"It's good. The kids working the beach and the shack are nice, and I love being outside in the sun," Laura said. She had her challenges with employees like Jason who failed to show up to work, but it was still a terrific way to spend her summer. After only a few weeks, she already wondered if she could go back to the confinement of the classroom with the same four gray walls, hard tile floor, rows of desks and the incessant bell schedule that dictated everything— including when she ate and when she went to the restroom.

Maybe she wasn't meant to try to churn out educated kids as if they were on a factory conveyor belt. As she walked through her high school during her free period and heard her colleagues engaging students and demonstrating excellence, she often felt they knew something she didn't. Had some gift or magic she didn't have.

She loved history. Loved reading about people who'd made a difference. The first female reporter. The first man to patent a mechanical breakthrough. The first group of hikers to climb a mountain. The women who'd pioneered chemical science.

Laura didn't expect to be on the pages of a book, but she did hope to make a tangible difference in the world.

"You're great with teenagers," Nicole said.

"I don't know about that," Laura said. "If I were such a genius with teenagers, my students wouldn't be watching the clock and asking really great questions like 'What time does this class end?' and 'Is this on the test?'"

"At least they're asking questions," Jane said. "Maybe it's part of their process."

"They don't have a process," Laura said. "They're required to take American history, but the great state of Indiana doesn't really care if they learn anything."

"You care," Nicole said.

Laura shrugged. She didn't want to ruin her sister's opinion of her, but she'd begun being honest with herself over the past year. "It gets harder every day. I'm not sure teaching high school is going how I thought it would. I used to watch those movies where high school teachers inspired their students and saved them from a life of crime and drugs. Students stood up to bullies and sang songs and got scholarships to their dream colleges. I loved those movies."

"Everyone loves those movies," Jane said. "Real life is harder."

"Maybe," Laura said. "And maybe I haven't found my true calling yet."

"Are you saying your true calling could be renting surfboards?" Nicole asked.

Laura put her hand over her heart. "I have seen my future," she said, grinning. "It's on a beach surrounded by beautiful vacationers and sweet families with children building castles and getting sand in every crevice of their bodies."

Jane clinked her smoothie glass against Laura's and Nicole's. "Let's drink to beautiful vacationers who come to town and give Cape Pursuit a reason to get out of bed in the morning."

They all sipped their smoothies, and Laura smiled as she thought of her reason for getting out of bed lately. The fire department and the chance to really give herself to a cause. She visualized herself rescuing someone from flames or resuscitating someone's loved one. Better than the someday hope of students realizing that the immortal words of the framers of the constitution have impacted their lives, firefighting was a true and present way she could give of herself.

Had her brother, Adam, known this feeling as he boarded the plane to head west and join his forest-fighting team for the summer? She hoped so. For the first time since his tragic death, Laura felt the leaden weight lift, just knowing he might have felt joy at the prospect of helping others just as she did now. Instead of sending him to his death by showing him that advertisement for firefighters, had she given him a chance to do something he loved, even for a brief time?

Wearing a pair of surgical gloves and carrying a garbage bag, Tony walked the sidewalks immediately surrounding the fire station. He picked up cigarette butts, a straw and plastic cup from a fast food restaurant, a soggy rolled up newspaper that must have been there since the rain three nights earlier, and a paper that looked like some kid's math homework.

"School's out, kid, so I can't help you," he said aloud. He continued down the next section of sidewalk framing the station. A few years earlier, he had led the committee that encouraged business owners and civic groups to adopt a section of town and keep it litter free. It was good for tourism in Cape Pursuit, but the visitors were also the reason why the litter force was needed. Virginia Beach just down the coastline got at least three million visitors a year, and Cape Pursuit got close to half a million with more hotels being built each year.

Tony wondered if he would need to create a sustainable plan for the increasing tourism. Would he need to add full-time members to his department and include volunteers more? He hoped he never saw the day when the Cape Pursuit Fire Department was understaffed or unable to respond in a life and death emergency.

Volunteers, like the ones coming in for training on this sunny Sunday morning, would add to the numbers and make a difference in saving someone's life in a staffing shortage. The many volunteers already on the books at the station were essential members of the department and were called in often during the busy season. Tony looked at his watch and stepped up his pace so he could finish cleaning up the sidewalks and gutters in his block. He wanted to be there when the volunteers showed up so he could assign them to experienced partners on their first day inspecting, stocking and cleaning the fleet of emergency vehicles.

He would pair up with one of the new trainees to teach the details of a good inspection, and he'd already told the other guys on duty they would have a partner who needed to be shown the ropes.

The brothers, Richard and Oliver, were the first to arrive. "Got me out of going to church with my wife and in-laws," Oliver said when Tony thanked them for showing up early. "We started going to her church after we got married a few months ago, but I haven't gotten used to it yet. Even my in-laws couldn't complain I was missing the service when they learned what I was doing instead. I think they believe I'm going to be some kind of hero," Oliver said with a wry smile.

"You never know what the day will bring," Tony said as they walked into the station where the overhead garage doors were already open. Their footsteps on the concrete floor echoed through the quiet station. "Since you two are brothers, I'm going to assign you to two other brothers working this morning. My cousins Tyler and Kevin Ruggles. They give each other crap, but they've always got each other's backs."

"Heard that," Tyler said, coming around the back of the fire truck with a cup of coffee in his hand. He set the cup on the silver running board and held out his hand. "I'm the good brother, Tyler."

They shook hands as Tony introduced Tyler to Richard and Oliver. "I'm taking this truck today, and I hope my baby brother gets stuck with the rescue truck this week. Whatever poor sucker gets that one has to take every single piece of equipment out and test it. After the hydraulic jaws failed last week, we don't want to take a chance on anything else."

"I'll do that one."

Tony and the other four men turned and saw Laura behind them.

"Bad deal," Kevin said, coming out of the bunk room. "If I heard you right. I'll work with you, but I suggest we grab either the tanker or the grass fire truck. It'll leave you more time to practice with the ladders and get comfortable carrying stuff up them."

"I can climb a ladder," Laura said. "I clean out the gutters on my parents' two-story house three times a year and carry all the yuck down in a bucket."

Kevin shrugged. "We can do the rescue truck, but don't say I didn't warn you."

"I'll work with Laura on that one," Tony said.

He saw Laura's quick glance and wondered what she thought of his offer. He didn't know himself why he had offered, except that he often did the hard jobs as a way of showing leadership. He wouldn't let Laura gut out the worst job without him. If his conscience said he was wrong to want to help and protect her, he reminded himself he would have and should have done the same for any of the new recruits foolish or dedicated enough to grab the toughest job.

"If you'll set up the ladders and help the volunteers take turns practicing," he said to Kevin, "when you get done doing a truck with one of these guys."

"That's a way better deal," Kevin said. "No offense, Laura."

She smiled at her future brother-in-law. "None taken. But it's going to be hard to make you look like a hero when I tell my sister this story."

Kevin laughed. "She was going to find me out eventually. Probably better before the wedding."

Tony found the clipboard for the rescue truck and gave it to Laura. "I'll be over in a few minutes after I assign everyone a partner."

He was glad the main attack pumper was in the way and he couldn't see Laura as she went to the rescue truck on the other side. One by one, all the volunteers arrived and Tony found them partners. Some of the trucks were easier to inspect than others, and that would mean more time on the ladders for those trainees. How confident was Laura in her ability to climb and carry heavy equipment? For that matter, he thought, as he looked at all the other members of the class, how confident were any of them?

It wasn't about the physical demands of the job. Firefighters and rescuers could be affected by tragedies on the job and in their personal life. No one was immune to trauma, and he wondered how the loss of her brother in a fast-moving forest fire would affect Laura if she was faced with her own fire. Would her past endanger her or someone else? It was his job to keep everyone safe, and allowing himself to care about her in a different way from the other firefighters could end badly. He reminded himself that Laura Wheeler was just another one of the firefighters under his command.

When everyone was assigned, Tony ducked around the main pumper and found Laura with the hood up on the rescue truck. She was standing on the front bumper leaning into the engine as if she was searching for something.

"It's on your right. Yellow," Tony said. He stood on the driver's side with his hands on the edge of the hood. He wanted to jump in and check the oil himself.

"Found it," she said. Tony handed her a shop rag. She appeared to know what she was doing. She replaced the dipstick, reported the level of wiper fluid was fine, tugged on the belts and hopped down from the bumper. She wiped her hands on the rag and cocked her head as she looked at him.

"Items one, two and three out of five thousand," she said, smiling.

"I think there are only five hundred things on the check sheet," he said. "I tried to condense it so I didn't scare people away."

Laura picked up the clipboard and ran her finger down the list. "You didn't have to offer to help me after I'd opened my big mouth to take the worst job."

"It's a big job, but not a terrible one. And it will be good experience for you to see everything we have in case we're out on a run and it's needed. Besides, you gave me an opportunity to look like a good leader by jumping in and getting my hands dirty."

"You are a good leader," Laura said.

Tony hated to admit how flattering her words were. There was something about her that made him want her admiration.

"I'm a work-in-progress like everyone else," he said.

"But you must be a pretty good work."

He shouldn't let her assessment of his merits affect him, but he'd have to be a stone statue not to enjoy her matter-of-fact approval. He'd heard it from other people, but coming from Laura, it felt especially nice.

He had to be careful of that feeling.

"Then I better keep earning it," he said.

"We'll start on the driver's side and pull out all the extrication equipment. Airbags, hydraulic jacks, saws and all kinds of things that can destroy a car in a hurry if you're trying to get someone out."

"Is this truck mostly for car accidents?"

"Often. We usually roll it along with the ambulance when we get called to an accident if we have the manpower. We use it for fires, too. When we get inside, you'll see extra air tanks and supplies for containing hazardous materials. We also keep bottled water and some food in here."

"In case there's no one available to bring you coffee in the middle of the night," Laura said. Her voice was soft and Tony saw a hint of the vulnerability he'd noticed the previous summer. "My sister told me about her adventure with Jane the night that Kevin saved the family's cat."

Tony vividly remembered the house fire a few doors down from Nicole's place. A family had lost their home but not their lives that night. He'd seen many nights like it, but what he remembered most was Nicole and Jane showing up out of the darkness with coffee and blankets. Despite her brother's death by fire, Nicole had come to help. Tony realized what strength that must have taken, and he wondered if Laura had the same—or even greater—resilience.

"Those are the best nights," Tony said. "And Kevin got way too much credit for saving the cat. He found it hiding under the truck after the fire was over, but the family considered him a hero."

Laura laughed and rolled up one of the doors and started at the bottom, pulling things out. "Should we just do one cabinet at a time in case an emergency comes in?" she asked. "I'd hate to have everything dragged out all over the floor if somebody gets in an accident."

"Good plan," Tony agreed.

As Laura took each item out, she checked it against the list on the clipboard. She had to ask what some of the tools were for, and Tony took his time explaining. Truck inspection followed by breakfast was usually over in a few hours, but he had all day and seeing each piece of equipment for himself was a good idea. He had the ultimate responsibility for everything that happened and every life that was jeopardized by equipment or training failure.

They moved on to the second cabinet, and Tony stepped away for a moment to check on how things were going. His cousins had helped while he was preoccupied with the rescue truck inspection. Kevin gave him a questioning glance. "You didn't have to take a truck, and I'll be glad to finish that for you if you want. Mine won't take long, and I know you're anxious to supervise the ladder training yourself."

"It's okay," Tony said. "If I do it myself, I won't have to try to read your lousy handwriting on the logs."

Kevin laughed. "Suit yourself."

As Tony walked back to where Laura knelt on the station floor surrounded by equipment and tools, he didn't think he was suiting himself. It would be a lot easier to keep his distance from Laura. He felt as if he had to tread carefully, knowing what had happened to her brother…even though she had signed up for this job. Rather than say the wrong thing, the safer bet would be to say as little as possible.

But he couldn't do that. Being a leader

meant he had to be as involved with his people as much as keeping them safe required. And he had to keep Laura safe—for her family who had already suffered a loss to the fire service.

CHAPTER SIX

LAURA LOOKED DOWN from the top of the ladder. With her elbow hooked over the rain gutters hanging off the roof of the Cape Pursuit fire station, she took a moment to enjoy the view of the ocean beyond the neighboring rooftops.

She also needed a moment to catch her breath after carrying a heavy length of fire hose up twenty feet. Gavin had timed her ascent, and he gave her a thumbs-up when she reached the top.

"Ten seconds," he called from the ground. "Not bad for a rookie."

"What's good for a rookie?" she asked.

"Twelve," he said, grinning and shading his eyes as he looked up at her. "You're making the rest of your class look bad. You'll have to sleep with one eye open if you make enemies."

"Luckily, I'm not sleeping with any of you," Laura yelled down.

Tony stepped out of the fire station just as she spoke. He looked from Gavin to her and back to Gavin, his expression stony.

"Volunteer slumber party at my house," Diane said. "I told you guys I was an empty nester. I'm warning you, I like to stay up late baking and you can't say no to my rhubarb pie without offending me."

Laura shot Diane a smile of appreciation at her attempt to knock down the awkwardness hanging like smoke in the air.

"Let's try climbing ladders while wearing turnout gear," Kevin said. "It's a hot day, and it will be good experience for you to see what thirty pounds of heavy clothing and an air tank will do to you. Adrenaline helps, but those extra pounds remind you fast that they're there."

Laura climbed down the ladder using a steady motion, always keeping one hand on a rung. She knew the ladder rules from her book and it was reiterated by Gavin that they were important, and the deliberate motion also helped focus her mind. She had a strong goal for the first time in two years, and she wouldn't let anything derail her. Even the strange feeling in her chest when she was alone with Tony, talking with him as if he was just a man and she was just a woman.

But they weren't. Their relationship had to be strictly business.

As she had inspected the massive rescue truck with Tony, she had chosen to consider it a giant utility closet on wheels to make it seem less intimidating. Would she learn to use all those tools in only six weeks? Although she wouldn't admit it even to her sister, Laura worried she would face off with an emergency she was unprepared for, and it was wrong to put her desire to add meaning to her life by serving others in front of the responsibility she was taking on.

The only thing she could do was to make certain she learned everything Tony and the other firefighters said. Commitment demanded it, and she already knew the cost firefighters could pay when they were caught by surprise.

She had to be better prepared than her brother had been.

Laura watched Kevin demonstrate how to arrange the turnout pants around the boots so he could step in fast, pull up the pants, shrug into the heavy coat and be ready in just seconds. He made it look easy, but when the new trainees tried, Marshall got his foot caught and had to use Brock's shoulder to keep himself from falling. Diane stepped into the boots, but the pants were so tall they came up to almost shoulder level.

Everyone laughed, including Tony, who had gone into the station but reemerged carrying an armload of helmets.

"It takes practice," he said.

"And you want us to climb ladders in these outfits?" Richard asked.

Kevin nodded. "And drive trucks, perform CPR and rescue cats in trees."

When Kevin mentioned cats, Tony glanced over at Laura and his eyes were full of laughter. Laura smiled back, enjoying the moment of camaraderie. His eyes held hers a moment longer than necessary, and she felt her cheeks heat as she quickly looked away.

"I better try this again," Marshall said. "I can't believe this is the hardest part of the day."

Laura noticed that Allen didn't join in with the self-deprecatory humor. He attacked each task as if he had to prove he was able. She thought it must be exhausting to always feel as if you're on trial, and she'd known students who strutted and offended as a result. Maybe Allen would crack a smile when he got more comfortable. Though Skip didn't say much, he also jumped into the boots and ladder drills as if his future depended on it. He didn't seem as if he was trying to impress anyone. Instead, Laura saw youthful zeal. Refreshing passion directly applied.

The borrowed boots Laura stepped into were much too large, but she managed to tug on her turnout pants, buckle the coat and walk with clunky efficiency over to the concrete where Tony had laid out the helmets.

"I'll help you adjust it so it stays on your head," Gavin said. He demonstrated how the straps and buckles worked and helped with fittings. "It's important to get it on securely because it won't do you any good if it falls off."

Laura saw Tony give Gavin an approving nod. When all eight recruits were suited up, Gavin asked for volunteers to go through the weighted ladder climbing exercise again.

Laura held up one hand. "I'll go first and get it over with," she said.

"You can go up the first time without the hose," Gavin said. "It might be a good idea to get used to the feel of the boots and turn-out gear."

She considered a trial run, but she was already hot and her muscles were being taxed. She wasn't kidding about getting it over with. "I'll take a chance and go big," Laura said. She slung the heavy length of rope over her right shoulder and started up the ladder. She wasn't going to do it in ten seconds this time. Instead, she concentrated on being strong and steady so she got her classmates started off with some confidence. If she missed a rung and bounced all the way down, it might demoralize the whole group, whom she was already starting to like and feel connected with. It would also draw attention to her in a way she didn't want.

She passed the halfway point and paused to look down through the rungs. Tony stood directly below her and looked up at her. Was he planning to catch her if she fell, or was he assessing her technique? She shifted her grip to the next rung up and tried to hang on tight even though her gloves were too big and an inch of extra fabric stuck out from each of her fingertips.

If she planned to become part of the department, she hoped one of the next phases would include finding gear that would fit. At least she was tall so the jacket didn't hang down past her knees as it did on Diane and Brock.

"It's not a test," Tony said. "You don't have to go all the way to the top today."

Laura didn't break her stride as she counted the last five rungs and touched the edge of the roof with one hand as she heard cheering from her friends on the ground.

"You can drop the hose," Tony called. "You don't have to carry it down."

Laura hitched the hose up on her shoulder and tightened her grip as she backed down the ladder. She tested each rung with her foot in the bulky boot to make sure her step was centered. She would not slip. She would not falter. She would not fail with ten pairs of eyes on her.

When she put one booted foot on the concrete, she felt the weight of the hose disappear from her shoulder and she realized Tony had lifted it away.

"Nice work," Tony said quietly so only she could hear. "That's a lot harder than most people think, and you don't have to prove yourself on your first try." He smiled at her. "Pace yourself. That's an order."

Before she could ask him if he was going to show such concern for everyone else, Tony had moved over to the other ladder set up and was helping Marshall get the hose balanced on his shoulder.

"You have to distribute your weight," Tony said. "I remember my first time hauling hose up a ladder at an actual fire. The ladder was wet, my boots were wet and I went for a heck of a ride. It wasn't my finest hour."

Okay, Laura thought. Tony's solicitude wasn't just about her. She took off her gloves and shoved them in the pocket of her turnout coat. It was incredibly hot on the white glaring concrete, and the heavy clothes and exertion made her feel as if she were burning up. She unbuckled her coat and swiped damp hair away from her face.

"Go inside and get something cold to drink," Tony said, appearing right next to her. He lifted her coat off her shoulders and removed it.

"I'm fine," she said. "I want to watch my classmates make it to the top of the ladder."

"You will. After you get a bottle of cold water out of the fridge in the breakroom."

Laura narrowed her eyes at him. "I can take care of myself."

"I'm sure you can. But when you're here, I take care of you," he said, his voice so low no one else could have heard it, especially with the sounds of Marshall grunting and scraping his way up the ladder and the spectators cheering him on. Laura felt a shiver run through her, despite the heat, as Tony's intense blue eyes assessed her as if she were valuable to him. No one had made her feel important in a long time, and it was a powerful sensation.

"I watch out for you and everyone else on the department," he said. "It's my job."

Laura glanced over and saw Diane giving her a concerned look. It probably seemed as if Tony was admonishing her, the way he stood close and spoke so only she could hear. Laura shot a smile at her new friend and turned on her heel to go into the station. Her boot gripped the ground and she wobbled, but she righted herself quickly and walked as smoothly as she could in the over-size clothes.

She went straight to the breakroom and opened the fridge. There was an entire case of bottled water, and she grabbed ten bottles, shoving them into the big square pockets of her turnout pants and holding four in her hands. When she got outside, she went around to everyone and handed out cold bottles. She got to Tony last and handed him a bottle from her pocket.

"You need to stay hydrated, too," she said. "After you."

He waited until Laura had opened her bottle and taken a long drink before he did the same.

"It's hard going back to work after a day off," Nicole said as Laura shared counter space in the kitchen and spread peanut butter on her toast. "Even though I love my job at the art gallery."

Laura leaned against the counter and took a bite of her toast. "I could barely make myself go to school last year. I had morning bus duty."

"Whatever that is, it sounds awful."

"It was my job to stand outside and watch kids get off the school buses." She paused to sip her coffee. "It was okay in the early fall and late spring. But the six months in between made me loathe winter for the rest of my life."

"They needed help getting off buses?" Nicole asked.

"I'm supposed to make sure they don't smoke or fight in front of the building, but they never even looked at me," Laura said. "They stepped off those buses as if they were walking through waist-deep mud. They don't look left or right, don't hear you when you try to sound chipper and wish them a good morning. They just haul their heavy backpacks full of everything but homework into the building."

"So they don't cause trouble?" Nicole said, smiling encouragingly. "Maybe that's not such a bad duty."

"Do you remember Indiana winters?"

"I'm trying to forget them," Nicole said. "I love Mom and Dad, but they're going to have to come here if they want to see me during the winter months. I'm done with snow."

"Great. You left me behind to fill their lonely evenings and weekends," Laura said.

Nicole's expression sobered and she put a hand on Laura's arm. "I'm sorry. I didn't think of it like that. And you don't have to babysit them. You have a right to your own life."

It would have been the perfect time to tell her sister why she felt so guilty about Adam's death, but Laura couldn't make herself. She hadn't admitted to anyone that she had been the one to tell Adam about the firefighting job, and maybe there was no point in it. She couldn't bring Adam back.

"Anyway," Laura said, trying to lighten her tone, "those winter mornings make summer days on the beach look even brighter. And I have plenty of summer left."

Nicole sucked in her lower lip, a sign that she had something on her mind.

"What?" Laura asked.

"Just wondering about your…uh…volunteering at the fire station."

"Wondering how it's going or wondering if I'm going to keep going?" Laura asked.

"Both."

"It's going great, and I'm going to another class tonight. This one's on hydraulics and the science behind water movement."

"That doesn't sound too dangerous," Nicole commented.

"Having a good water supply is a key element in fighting fires."

Nicole blew out a breath and stirred sugar into her coffee. "I've heard about that from Kevin, although he usually keeps the shop talk to a minimum. I think he's afraid to tell me everything about his job for fear I'll be a runaway bride and go marry a nice safe man who owns his own carpet cleaning service."

"If that's what he thinks, he hasn't figured out how strong you are," Laura said.

"No one knows how strong they are until they have to be," Nicole said. "It would be nice if we could get through life without having to answer that question."

Laura swallowed, unsure how to respond. As the months passed and added up to two years since their younger brother had died, they had spoken of him less and less. Their parents hadn't moved very far beyond the initial pain and shock. Laura had blamed it on their static situation. Same home, same cars, same jobs, same bench in the entryway where Adam had always left his shoes in the way. Nicole had physically moved away, and emotionally opened her heart in the bravest way possible. Could Laura do the same? Spending the summer in Cape Pursuit and facing her brother's death in the most direct manner possible was her way of finding out.

Laura hugged her sister. "I'm going to test my strength by riding my bike to work. If anyone asks, I'm planning to pretend it was uphill at least one way."

"You'll get home before dark?"

"Long before. I only work until early afternoon, and then I plan to come home and read up to get ready for my class tonight."

"You don't have to be the best student in the class," Nicole said, laughing.

"Yes, I do."

Laura took her bicycle down from its hooks in her sister's garage and pedaled down the street. It was early morning in Cape Pursuit, and most of the tourists were in their hotels sleeping off late-night dinners and drinks, and recovering from sunburns from the previous day. As she rode past the high-rise hotels facing the water and separated by parking lots and restaurants, she smelled eggs, bacon and coffee, and heard car doors slamming as a family stuffed their luggage into a minivan for a return trip home.

The last day of vacation and the long slow drive back to reality had always bummed Laura out when she was a kid. Lucky for her, she thought, she was spending an entire summer doing what felt like a vacation. She had free reign of her sister's house. She had a fun job in the sunshine, a bike, a car and a new passion.

What she didn't have was much pride in her decision-making over the past year or so. She'd wasted time feeling sorry for herself, even though it was her brother who had lost his life. She'd squandered her emotions on pointless dates with men as shallow as mud puddles. Worst of all, she hadn't confided in her sister as much as she should have. She hadn't told Nicole how seriously she was considering not going back to her second-floor classroom in the sixty-year-old building in Indianapolis.

She'd made friends with the mouse that

lived in her classroom's supply closet, accepted the fact that there was always a line at the copier when she was getting an assignment ready at the last minute, and learned to live with teenagers whose emotions were like driving in stop-and-go traffic. What she couldn't accept was the fact that the kids didn't want her help. Didn't need her. Wouldn't let her fix their problems for them, no matter how much she wanted to.

Adam had needed her. She was closest to him in age, and she had tutored him through his high school classes. Her parents knew how much Laura had helped her brother, and that was the reason her mother suggested she should become a teacher. Always looking to please her parents and earn her slice of their approval as the middle child, Laura had seized on the idea and gotten her teaching degree.

She remembered Adam proudly telling her friends at graduation that he had been her inspiration. That was true. And now he was gone.

But she had a new purpose in life. If there were flames, she'd douse them. If someone was trapped in a car, she'd get them out. She wasn't naive enough to think she'd save everyone, but the trying would feel more honorable, measurable, practical.

Laura pedaled her bike past boutiques that wouldn't open for a few hours and miniature golf courses that wouldn't pick up business until the afternoon. She heard a siren behind her and perked up her ears. It was growing closer, and it was accompanied by the roar of a powerful engine. She pulled over and parked her bike so she could stay out of the way and also watch the emergency vehicle go past.

It was the main attack pumper followed by the rescue truck and an ambulance. At least two men were visible in the front seats of each vehicle, and she could see they were wearing turnout gear. Laura admired the skill of driving a giant truck encumbered by boots and heavy clothes.

She had a rush of adrenaline and wished she could follow them, even though Tony had lectured them against that on the first night of class. He'd told them they couldn't show up at emergency scenes until they were fully trained, and he'd shared stories of bystanders who had good intentions but bad results.

Still, Laura knew where every tool was on the rescue truck after Sunday's inspection. She could be helpful.

She also had a responsibility to her job at the beach where people counted on her to make their day fun and safe. So, she watched the first two trucks go past. When the ambulance got close, someone stuck his arm out the window and waved vigorously at her. She didn't have time to see who it was, but she waved back, hoping whoever it was would notice her return wave in the side mirror.

A feeling of belonging swept over her as she stood for a moment and watched the rescue vehicles disappear down the long street of tourist attractions, lodgings and restaurants. After only a week of training for the Cape Pursuit Fire Department, she already felt as if she were part of something important that could change her life.

CHAPTER SEVEN

"JASON CALLED IN AGAIN," the girl at the beach shack counter said as soon as Laura came through the back door.

"Sick?" Laura asked.

"Didn't say," Rebecca said. "Tell me again why you haven't fired him."

"Well, for starters, he hasn't shown up for me to fire him. I hate doing that kind of thing over the phone."

Rebecca laughed. "You're not going to have much of a choice. And we don't have a lifeguard for part of the beach for the afternoon shift."

"We'll cover it."

"We were already down a person because Chelsea is on a college visit today. She's visited fifteen colleges, I swear."

"Sometimes it's hard to find just the right one." Laura reviewed the staffing calendar. "Jordan was going to help us out in here this afternoon, but I'll run this place myself all day and send Jordan out to the guard chair." She closed the calendar. "Problem solved."

"The problem is solved if you don't mind working a double," Rebecca said. "I would stay over a little while and help you, but I have to be home to watch my little brother tonight. I promised my mom."

"It's okay. I think I can still make it to my fire training class on time, and I brought my books with me to study so I can go right from here to there."

"I thought you were a teacher."

"I am. But even teachers need to study."

She had read through the entire first module of the training book, stopping frequently to put notes into a document. Out of habit, she always read nonfiction with pauses to summarize the text. She found herself thinking of guiding questions to help her remember important facts. She wrote summaries and bullet points at the end of each section and color-coded them on her computer screen. If there was going to be a test, she would be ready for it.

"I mean, I thought you were a teacher, so why are you taking fire training classes?"

Rebecca said. "Don't get me wrong, my Aunt Diane is glad you're in the class, too, so she's not the only girl. But she doesn't have a full-time job like you do. Are you planning to quit being a teacher?"

Laura shrugged, not feeling like explaining herself to a girl ten years younger who would have to make up her own mind about things. It was drilled into the minds of educators. You can be friendly to teenagers, but you're not their friend. You don't unload on them. They unload their problems on you. "I like to improve my mind during the summer," she said using a fake haughty voice and knowing it would kill any further questions.

"Uh," Rebecca said. "That's what all adults say."

"They're right."

For the first day since she'd arrived in Cape Pursuit, Laura watched the clock on her job. She cheerfully rented beach equipment and went through the next week's schedule to remove Jason and lessen the impact of his unreliability. She restocked the water and sports drinks for the lifeguards, swept the sand out of the beach hut and hauled a broken beach umbrella to the dumpster.

All she wanted to do was ride home, change into something appropriate for class, have a cold drink while reviewing the fire training manual and give herself plenty of time to drive to the station. As it was, she would barely make it. The beach shack and lifeguard stations closed at seven o'clock and signs would be posted for the rest of the evening, warning swimmers to enter the water only at their own risk.

Her class at the station started at 7:00 p.m.

"Nicole," Laura said when her sister picked up the phone. "Huge favor."

Nicole pulled into the city lot closest to the beach shack at 6:50 p.m. and didn't even bother to park. Laura dove into the passenger seat and reached into the back for the clothes she'd asked her sister to bring.

"I closed the beach shack ten minutes early, but I don't think anyone will care. The lifeguards can finalize the night closing without me."

As her sister drove, Laura pulled a lightweight blue shirt over her head and removed the shirt she had on underneath. She wiggled out of her beach shorts and pulled on a pair of jeans without taking off her seat belt.

"Should I ask how you gained experience changing your clothes in the front seat of a moving car without exposing yourself?" Nicole asked.

"Cross-country practice. We did it on the bus all the time."

"Good answer." Nicole pulled up in front of the fire station.

"You're the best," Laura said. "I know you don't love me joining the fire department, but thanks for coming through for me in an emergency. I think I have two minutes to spare."

Nicole nodded toward the station where Tony stood outside, arms crossed over his chest. "Your instructor doesn't look impressed, but he didn't see the calisthenics you went through to get here on time."

"I don't know what he thinks of me," Laura whispered. She slid out, opened the back door and grabbed her books off the seat.

Nicole put a hand on her sister's arm and leaned close. "What do you think of him?"

The two sisters had shared a bedroom and plenty of secrets all their lives, and they'd become even closer since they'd lost Adam. But

Laura didn't know how to answer the question honestly. She spent a third of her time with Tony listening intently so she'd learn from him, a third of her time admiring him for his attitude, leadership and service, and the remaining third wondering what it would be like to run her fingers through his short blond hair and touch a kiss to his highly forbidden lips.

"To be determined," Laura said.

"Wait," Nicole said.

"What?"

"Your shirt's on inside out."

Laura looked down. "Rats. But there's nothing I can do about it now."

"Just wow them with your intelligence and they won't notice."

Laura flashed a grin at her sister and shut the door. She composed her expression and steadied her breathing as she walked across the wide concrete apron that separated the station from the street.

"We need to talk about safety," Tony said without any greeting at all.

"Nicole's not a bad driver, although she did make a few rolling stops to get me here on time," Laura said. "Isn't class about to start? Shouldn't we get inside?"

"I didn't like what I saw this morning," Tony said.

He waited, looking dour. It was the same treatment Laura had given students when she asked them to step into the hallway. She let them stew a moment and then asked them if they knew why she wanted to see them. Sometimes her tactic was met with begrudging silence, and sometimes they spilled their guts about infractions she hadn't even known they committed.

"You'll have to be more specific," she said. "Was your breakfast undercooked? Maybe there was bird poop on your windshield?"

He didn't crack a smile.

"Your reflection in the bathroom mirror frowned at you and made you feel uncomfortable?" she suggested. "I know how that might feel."

"I saw you on your bike when I went by on the way to a fire."

"That was you! Were you the one who waved at me?"

"No."

"Okay," Laura said. "So you saw me. I pulled over, just like I was supposed to."

"I wish you would wear a helmet."

"Is *that* what this is about?"

"Laura," he said, putting a hand on her elbow. "Being in the fire service changes you. Things you wouldn't have noticed stick out. Worries most people don't have get you right in the heart. I can't walk into a public place without looking for fire exits and counting sprinkler heads. I can't see a carload of teenagers pass me without knowing what a wrong move on a rainy road can do."

Laura swallowed, sobered by Tony's expression. He dropped his hand from her elbow.

"I didn't like the fact that you had no helmet on, but you looked as if you were ready to jump on our trucks and go with us as we went by." His serious expression lightened. "I did like that."

Laura almost smiled at the hint of approval from Tony, and it validated her sense of belonging to the Cape Pursuit Fire Department.

"SECURING THE SCENE," Tony said. "I'm skipping ahead to chapter ten because I think this should be taught earlier in the course."

He watched as the class members shuffled their books and searched for the chapter. Laura was the only person who seemed unfazed by the change. Her book had colored tabs sticking up, marking the chapters, he guessed. She flipped to chapter ten and sat back, waiting, pen in hand.

"You can be the best firefighter in the world, you can be a champion at giving first aid, but if you don't keep yourself safe out there, you can't help anyone," Tony said.

Laura cocked her head and narrowed her eyes just a little, and Tony imagined she was thinking this was a continuation of his lecture about the bike helmet. It was, but not entirely.

Everyone in the class had managed to find chapter ten, and the room fell silent. Tony didn't consider himself a gifted teacher or a great storyteller, so he usually stuck with the facts. In this case, the facts were themselves a compelling tale.

"I think I already told you my dad was the fire chief here, so you can imagine I got a lot of lectures about safety when I was a kid. When I was invited to stay the night at another kid's house, sometimes my dad said no and I didn't understand why until years later. We never had a live Christmas tree. There were no candles in our house. We didn't leave shoes or anything else blocking exits."

Diane and Oliver gave him sympathetic looks, but Skip raised one hand and said, "I know what you mean. My uncle was a major party pooper."

"I learned a lot from my dad," Tony continued. "And some of these lessons were hard. One time, we were driving home from a theme park. It had been a fun day, just my dad and me. It was dusk, and we were just coming into Cape Pursuit when a man on a bicycle rode into traffic and bounced off a car."

"Ouch," Allen said.

"Worse than ouch. We saw him fly up in the air and come down right on his head. It was ugly. He was in a heap on the painted line on the edge of the road. I thought he was dead for sure."

Despite the many terrible things he had seen since that day, Tony would never forget the details of that evening. He could remember the slant of the sun, the sound of the cars, the red shirt the man was wearing.

"What did you do?" Diane asked.

"My dad pulled over, put his flashers on and went to see if he could help the guy. There was blood coming out of his ears, and I didn't think even my hero dad could do anything. As I watched, a driver that obviously wasn't paying attention nearly ran over my dad and the injured guy."

Tony saw Laura's mouth open and her eyes widen.

"My dad went to the back of his truck, pulled out a reflective vest and put it on me and then struck a road flare and handed it to me. He told me to direct traffic around him and the guy on the ground and not to leave my post no matter what."

"How old were you?" Richard asked.

"About twelve. So I stood there with my road flare as my dad called for help on his radio. I waved my arms and diverted traffic, and it seemed like forever. Once, I heard the man moan, and I turned to see what was going on. I let down my guard and my flare, and a car whizzed close to Dad. He gave me a look I'll never forget, and I hurried back to my job."

"You were a brave kid," Brock said.

"Not as brave as my dad. He knew that poor man was going to die, and I don't think there was anything he could do about it. I stood there, waving at traffic and thinking I had the worst job in the world until I listened to what my dad was doing. He was sitting on the ground next to the guy, just talking to him. Telling him about what teams he thought would make it to the World Series. Which restaurants in town had good food. The best time of year for fishing along the coast."

The room was silent as everyone processed the sad story. Tony thought of his father's actions all the time when he was at emergency scenes. It takes bravery to face danger and ugly situations, but it takes a lot more to face a situation you can't do a thing about. In the face of a stranger's death alongside a road at dusk, his father had called up every scrap of his humanity to make sure that man didn't die like a lonely animal hit by a car.

"I thought Dad was the hero that day,"

he said. "But then I crept downstairs later that night and listened to him tell my mother about it. He told my mother that he wouldn't have come home alive if it hadn't been for me keeping him from getting hit by a car, too. He said I was the hero."

"Wow," Oliver breathed.

Tony sat on the edge of the desk. "I'm telling you this story because there are a lot of times you'll be asked, as new volunteers, to do jobs that don't seem important. You might be the person directing traffic around an accident or babysitting the radio in the station. You could get the unglamorous job of refilling air tanks in the rescue truck or hosing down a neighboring structure. But every job is important. And if the officer in charge tells you to do something, you have to do it to the best of your ability or someone could die."

He paused, letting a beat of silence pass in the heavy atmosphere.

"And if someone tells you to put on your helmet or your air pack, or if an officer tells you to get the hell out of someplace right now, you don't ask questions. You do it."

Laura's forehead wrinkled and her eyes

searched his face as if she expected to find a message there. He didn't even want to think about her getting hit by a car and lying crumpled on the edge of the road. Tony let out a long breath and moved behind his desk. He needed to get the evening's lesson back on track. He opened his book to chapter ten and looked out at the eight serious faces in the room. He knew he'd impressed upon them the importance of following orders, but there was a lot left to learn. Some of it they could learn from the book, but experience had a lot to show them.

"So," he said. "Now that I've shared the least warm and fuzzy childhood story possible, let's talk about how to decide if an emergency scene is safe and what to do about it. You've seen the trucks out there with flashing lights and other safety equipment. You'll have that with you in an emergency, and I sure hope you won't have to rely on a twelve-year-old to save your butt."

He pointed out various scenarios outlined in the chapter and gave some anecdotes that brought the text to life. As he spoke, Laura kept her attention on her book and took notes. She didn't look at him, and he was afraid he had hurt her with his harsh story. Only she would know it was, at least partly, directed at her.

But of all the people in the room who were aware that sometimes firefighters don't come home from trying to save someone, she knew it from the hardest lesson. Wanting to keep Laura safe made his job so much more difficult because he wanted to avoid the subject of her brother's death. His attraction to her made it even worse because letting feelings intrude in an emergency could mean everyone got hurt. It was an impossible and maddening paradox, and all he could think as he watched her take notes was that he would like to see her look up and smile.

CHAPTER EIGHT

NICOLE AND LAURA stood in front of Nicole's closet. They had an hour before they had to meet Kevin at the restaurant that would be catering Nicole and Kevin's wedding in just over a month. Kevin and Nicole had arranged to talk with the owner after a complimentary dinner where they could sample as many different entrées as there were people in their party.

Laura was excited about helping her sister plan her wedding, and it was one of the reasons she'd given her parents for spending the summer in Cape Pursuit. At twenty-five, she didn't have to justify her actions to her parents, but both she and Nicole felt a responsibility to be gentle on their mom's and dad's feelings after the loss of Adam. Laura had never talked about it specifically with her sister, but she knew that Nicole was very sensitive to their parents' lingering grief. Laura dreaded telling them about joining the volunteer fire department. Nicole had barely accepted it, and her parents would be worse.

"I think maybe a dress, but not necessarily a cocktail dress," Nicole said. "It's a nice restaurant, so I told Kevin he had to wear a shirt with buttons."

"That's not very specific," Laura said.

"It narrows the choices to three items in his wardrobe, and I'd be happy with any of them."

"Smart," Laura said. "Does his brother have to dress up, too?"

"About that," Nicole said. "I should have said something earlier, but Tyler can't come. He has to go to some event at his daughter's summer camp. It's the last day of the week-long camp and the kids are putting on a play for their parents. He didn't know about it until this week."

"That's okay," Laura said. "We can sample food without the best man. I'll volunteer to test his entrée."

Nicole pulled out a dress and held it against herself as she looked in the long mirror on the closet door. "So Kevin asked Tony to come along since he's also in the wedding party," she blurted out.

Laura felt a shiver of nervousness at the thought of having dinner with Tony. In a dress, in a social setting. She didn't want to upset her sister, though, so she shrugged. "I'm sure he'll have no trouble expressing an opinion about food."

"They're picking us up," Nicole said. "Kevin and Tony. I guess parking is limited at the restaurant during the busy tourist season, so it makes sense for us all to go together."

Laura shoved several dresses down the rack in the closet. "If we all ride in the car together, it'll seem like a double date," she said lightly. "I hope none of the other firefighters will be at the restaurant. They might think I'm wining and dining our instructor for a better grade."

"You don't need help with that," Nicole said. "And it's obviously not a date. You're both there to help us decide on appetizers and entrées. We'll have wedding cake at the reception, of course, so we don't have to choose a dessert tonight." Then Nicole put a hand on her chest and made a whooshing sound.

"Are you okay?" Laura asked, touching her sister's shoulder.

"Yes," Nicole said, fanning herself. "I can talk about the wedding without getting panicked, but once in a while it hits me. Like imagining my wedding cake being cut up and served as if it's the final statement. Like crossing the *t* and dotting the *i* on the marriage license. Serving the wedding cake. There's only one occasion for that in a girl's life."

"Not necessarily," Laura said. "You could have wedding cake on a Tuesday for no reason or on Thanksgiving, just to shake things up. A big tiered cake with a turkey on top. Maybe two turkeys if it's a wedding cake."

"No, you can't," Nicole said. "Wedding cake is sacred. It's a one-time deal."

"And you've already chosen the flavors and stuff, right? Like how tall and wide and how much fancy decoration and if there will be flowers on it?"

"Right," Nicole said, her hand still over her heart. "I picked out a picture in a book that I thought was just right. The bakery across from Sea Jane Paint is doing the cake. We went for pretty standard flavors because our friends—especially the firefighters— aren't exactly experimental with food. A big vanilla layer, a chocolate layer, a spice layer and the chocolate for the small one on top."

"That you'll save for your first anniversary," Laura said.

Nicole put both hands on her chest and breathed out slowly. "Yes. But I keep worrying about the silliest things like how my cat will adjust to Kevin's dog. What if Claudette hates Arnold?"

"You have to get a grip," Laura said. "You're not leaping off a bridge. You're getting married. And now I'm wondering about our efforts tonight. If this is a chocolate-and-vanilla crowd, maybe we don't have to overthink the catering menu too much."

"Kevin said they would be happy with hot dogs, baked potatoes and maybe an ice-cream machine."

"Ugh, that sounds like school lunch," Laura said. "I think we'll make excellent choices tonight, and I've already given Mom and Dad permission to spend all their saved-up wedding funds on you."

"You'll get married someday," Nicole said.

"We'll see about that." For the past two years, Laura hadn't thought much about her future. Getting through every day had been enough of a challenge. But seeing her sister's happiness and looking forward to every sunrise over the ocean had started to change her.

Unfortunately, she had her own heart-pausing fears about her sister's wedding. Her parents had cheerfully encouraged her to spend the first part of the summer with Nicole, preparing for the wedding, but they fully expected her to return to Indiana with them after the happy occasion. Laura hadn't told them about her temptation to quit her teaching job and that she had become more and more certain of the plan with each passing day.

She hadn't even told her sister, and now it was going to be a big drama that could overshadow Nicole's wedding. Laura didn't want to hurt her sister or anyone in her family. They'd all been through too much.

Nicole pulled a sleeveless rose-colored dress from her closet and picked up a pair of low-heeled sandals. She handed them to her sister. "You have the arms and the legs for this."

Laura laughed. "Thanks for saying that. What are you wearing?"

Nicole sorted through the rack and picked a sky blue dress with a V-neck and short sleeves. "This one. We're going to look fabulous for our double date."

"Ha," Laura said. "Very funny. I swear, if anyone shows up with a corsage, I'm driving myself to the restaurant and picking out the weirdest things on the menu for your reception."

An hour later, Nicole and Laura were waiting by the front door when Kevin pulled into the driveway in his new four-door pickup truck. To her horror, Laura watched both Kevin and Tony get out, each holding open a door for her and Nicole. Kevin kissed Nicole right before she got into the front passenger seat.

Tony said nothing as Laura got in the back and he closed the door. Laura really wished she had driven separately, because sitting next to Tony reinforced all the reasons she could not date him—and all the reasons it would be nice if she could. Where were all the other brave attractive men hiding? It didn't matter. She couldn't date a man who could potentially be her supervisor. It would be twelve kinds of awkward at the fire station, and she was afraid the other firefighters wouldn't take her seriously.

Kevin backed out of the driveway and he and Nicole chatted easily about their days. Laura risked a glance at Tony and he looked at her at the same time. He cleared his throat. "Did you get a new bike helmet yet?"

"I have one back home, in my parents' garage."

"It's not doing you any good there."

Laura wanted to say something sarcastic about the obviousness of Tony's statement, but then she remembered his story and pictured him at the tender age of twelve watching a man die from a head injury.

"I know," she said. "Cape Pursuit seems like a permanent vacation, and feeling the wind in my hair on the way to work completes the package."

Tony unbuttoned the cuffs on his blue oxford shirt and began rolling up his sleeves instead of answering her. He took his time, making neat, even folds up to his elbows.

Was it hot in the truck? Laura tried not to watch, but it was a fascinating glimpse into his mind. She knew he was irritated with her, and the last thing she wanted was for her potential fire chief to think she was sloppy about safety. But he held his lecture and rolled his sleeves with calm, deliberate hands.

Was that how he handled life? Everything? Calmly doing something instead of saying something he might regret? He had handled that day last summer when he drove her home to her sister's empty house and asked no questions as he gave her wet washcloths and pulled down the blinds in her bedroom.

She couldn't think about that day, or Tony, without feeling a deep vulnerability sweep over her. As if she had almost lost it and stepped back from the edge of the cliff just in time.

There were no cliffs this summer. A year had done her good, and she was much stronger than Tony probably thought.

"We had an interesting call earlier today," Tony said. "A man had a heart attack down in the cuddy cabin of a boat in the marina."

"Code?" Kevin asked, picking up the conversation from the front seat.

"Yes," Tony said. "It wasn't pretty. Had a heck of a time doing CPR and getting him off the rocking boat."

"Don't tell me my brother was on the call," Kevin said.

Tony laughed. "He was. That was the part that wasn't pretty. The patient will live, but Tyler may never be the same."

"Why not?" Laura asked.

"Kevin's brother is notorious for getting seasick. He never goes out on the rescue boat, and trust me, you don't want him to."

"So tell me what you did," Laura said. "For training's sake. If I had been there as a volunteer, what would I have been doing?"

"We might have sent you to the truck for supplies. Backboard, intubation kit. After you're with us a little bit longer, we might have had you down in the cuddy cabin doing compressions. You're light but strong."

Laura felt herself growing warm at his practical assessment of her physical attributes, and she didn't know what to say.

"I noticed that when you were climbing the ladders," Tony said. He tugged at the collar of his shirt. "Anyway, it's one of those situations you can train for, but you still never know what you're going to get."

"When are we doing CPR training in our class?"

"Next week."

"Good," Laura said. "I'm certified, but a refresher will be good."

"I like how you asked what you would have done. Remind me to tell everyone at the class next week about that. It's a useful skill, visualizing scenarios in advance and always thinking about what you would do."

"Right now," Kevin said, "I'm thinking of running through a drive-through on the way to the restaurant and getting a preemptive cheeseburger just in case it's all fancy stuff that doesn't look like food. I'm starving."

"See?" Tony said. "Kevin's a true professional."

They pulled into the restaurant, and Laura opened her door and slid out before Tony could come around the truck. Riding with him in the back seat had been strange enough. She'd tried not to notice how his blue shirt matched his eyes and how neatly combed his short blond hair was. Tried not to notice his navy blue socks with a narrow gold stripe and his dress shoes that were perfectly clean as if he had just shined them.

They walked side by side behind Kevin and Nicole, and the lady at the seating kiosk directed them to a cozy table in a nook by a window. Tony pulled out a chair for Laura and took the one right next to her. Kevin and Nicole sat across from them, looking like two people so in love that their chairs seemed to inch closer together. Laura glanced down at the three-inch gap between her seat and Tony's. She wasn't sure it was enough to remind her that the handsome, thoughtful man next to her was completely off-limits. If she wanted to be taken seriously as a firefighter and give her new life a chance, there was no way she could date the chief.

TONY WAITED UNTIL everyone else had chosen their entrées so he could pick something different. He'd volunteered to go last because he wasn't fussy about the food and would have been happy with the beef tips, chicken Marsala, lasagna or pork chops. He was glad the waitstaff seemed to be moving quickly, and they had already placed their drink and appetizer orders. The faster the evening went, the safer he would be from blundering into something he shouldn't say to Laura.

"While we wait," Nicole said. "You should tell me a funny story about growing up with Kevin. Something I don't already know."

He sipped his soda and smirked at his cousin over the rim of the glass. "Does she know about the haunted house?"

"Yep."

"And the broken arm?"

"Uh-huh. I already confessed everything embarrassing because I knew she'd hear it all from you or Tyler otherwise."

"You're no fun," Nicole said.

"Actually, we're in luck having your sister here," Kevin said. "I'll bet Laura can tell us something funny from your childhood."

"No way," Laura said. "Most of those stories would implicate me, too."

"So it would have to be a good story. Something not embarrassing," Tony suggested. The mood at the table was light and friendly, and he hoped to keep it that way. Sharing fun stories from childhood seemed a much safer topic than talking about Laura's new firefighting interest. Tony hadn't talked with Nicole directly about it, but he had the impression Laura's sister wasn't thrilled. Bringing up the day's ambulance run had been acceptable shoptalk in the truck, but the restaurant was a different atmosphere. Tony was careful to never talk about their calls in public because people who had suffered an emergency deserved privacy, and he never knew who could be listening.

Laura gave him a grateful smile. "Telling safe stories is a good idea, and we can all remain friends until at least the appetizer round. If you want a nice story, I could tell you about Nicole's love for animals. She was like a magnet for them. We always seemed to stumble on abandoned litters of kittens or lost puppies."

"And you adopted them?" Kevin asked.

"We always swore we would if we had our own houses, but our parents had different ideas. They were willing to accept two kittens born under our neighbor's back porch, and those cats lived to a respectable old age. They even let us keep the puppy we found under the slide on the school playground for a few days before Dad found someone at work to take her," Laura said.

"The raccoons didn't go so well," Nicole said.

"Raccoons?" Kevin asked.

"We found a bunch of babies whose mother had been hit by a car. They weren't all that friendly, but we felt sorry for them." Nicole said.

"And you took them home?" Tony asked. "I'm guessing that didn't turn out well." Even though he could already imagine the disaster that probably ensued, he liked the idea of Laura and her sister taking in lost woodland creatures. The sisters had big hearts and a desire to help.

Laura nodded. "Our fatal mistake was not knowing they're nocturnal and like to creep around at night. Plus hiding them in the bathtub wasn't the best idea. I was only eight, but Nicole was old enough to know better."

"I was ten," Nicole said, laughing. "And the bathtub was your idea."

Tony laughed. "I'm picturing this."

"I thought it would be cleaner that way," Laura said. "They were pretty smelly."

"What happened?" Kevin asked.

"Mom got up in the night to use the bathroom," Nicole said. "The baby raccoons scattered, everyone was screaming and we couldn't remember how many babies there had been in the first place. We thought we had them all but we found one in the hall closet the next day."

"And what did your parents do?" Kevin asked.

"They were furious," Nicole said. "I remember Dad saying something about rabies and distemper and Mom getting out the vacuum cleaner as if that would erase any traces of wild animal from the shag carpet in the hallway."

"Adam was so sad he'd missed all the excitement when he got home," Laura said wistfully, and Tony noticed the hitch in her voice. "He was only gone for two nights on a Cub Scouts thing, and he was sure mad we didn't keep any of the baby raccoons for him."

"I think it was very sweet of you to try to save them," Kevin said. He kissed Nicole on the temple and looked at her as if he wouldn't mind her bringing home baby snakes or lions. It created an awkward tension at the table, and Tony was glad when their combination plate of appetizers arrived. Everyone else dug in, but Tony waited.

"Aren't you having any?" Laura asked.

"I'll eat whatever's left. I like just about everything."

"I'll bet it comes in handy at the fire station."

Tony nodded as he took two items that remained on the plate. "And at the family dinner table."

"Do you have brothers and sisters?" Laura asked.

"Two younger sisters," he said. "One is going to med school and wants to be an ophthalmologist and the other one works at the day care center."

"She must like little kids," Laura said. "That's a tough job."

"Tiffany had a son her senior year of high school. He's four now, and the job has been a blessing because she can take him to work with her."

"So you're an uncle," Laura said.

"I try my best. If we're lucky, my nephew, Brandon, will decide to join the fire service when he's older."

When their entrées arrived, Tony waited until everyone had their food. It all looked and smelled delicious, and he didn't see how

Nicole and Kevin were going to choose. Laura had chosen the baked chicken over a bed of homemade noodles, and Tony had to admit it looked better than his pork chops.

"Want to try some of mine?" Laura offered to everyone at the table. "These noodles are delicious. Remember Grandma's homemade noodles?" she asked her sister. "I used to wonder why Mom never made those, but then I watched a cooking show about making your own noodles and realized Mom didn't have all day."

Tony considered the thick homemade noodles heaped on Laura's plate, but eating off the plate of any woman would be too personal. It would be especially inappropriate because she was one of his trainees. He hated to admit to himself how special she was becoming to him, and crossing even the narrowest line would make it hard to go back.

"Try some," Laura said. She shoved her plate so close to his that they almost touched. She looked at him expectantly, and when he glanced across the table at Kevin and Nicole, they were also waiting for him to make a move.

"Thanks," he said, quickly forking a few

noodles onto his plate. He was comfortable being a leader at the fire station but not so happy to be the object of everyone's attention here. Did Nicole and Kevin suspect how he was beginning to feel about Laura? If he was lucky, the dinner would be over soon, and he knew there wouldn't be dessert tonight because Kevin had already told him dessert would be wedding cake.

All he had to do was keep a professional layer between him and Laura for a little while longer and then on the ride home and he could forget how nice she looked, how sweet she smelled sitting next to him, and how he'd been unable to resist eating off her plate. For a man accustomed to a dangerous job, he wasn't prepared for this.

"I heard the city got a grant to expand the beach access near the beach shack," Kevin said.

Nicole nodded. "Jane told me. Council wants to begin construction later this summer after they bid out the project. She said the plans call for better handicapped accessibility, more parking and even some mixed retail space."

"It should be great," Laura said. "We

heard rumors, but I haven't seen any official plans."

"Jane said the timing was a shame because it won't be done by the time school starts and the beach quiets down," Nicole said, directing her words to her sister. "But it gives you a good excuse to come back and visit us next summer."

Laura put her fork down deliberately and lined it up neatly with the side of her plate. Tony sensed a shift in the table atmosphere. Maybe it was Laura's raised chin or the long pause before she replied to her sister, but there was definitely something in the air.

"Maybe I'll be around to see it before then," Laura said.

"Oh?" Nicole asked.

"Maybe I'm not totally sure I'm going back to teaching."

"But you have to. It's your job," Nicole said.

"It *was* my job. I have until the last day of July to bail out of the school year without losing my teaching license. I'm not sure I want to go back to the tenth-grade classroom where the kids spend all their time sneaking looks at their phones or wishing they were seniors. Maybe I'll stick around here."

Tony was stunned. Was Laura serious? Did her work at the fire station have anything to do with it? He didn't want to be responsible for completely upending her life.

"What are you talking about?" Nicole said. "You can't just quit a decent job and move to Cape Pursuit."

"That's what you did last summer."

Tony expected Nicole to argue that her situation was different. He knew Nicole had left her job in Indiana and made a temporary move to Cape Pursuit to stay with her friend Jane and work in Jane's art gallery. He had no idea how permanent she had planned for it to be, but he was glad for Kevin's sake that Nicole was here to stay.

Instead of arguing, Nicole sat perfectly still in her chair, her eyes a little shiny. Kevin put his hand over hers. Tony glanced at Laura, hoping he wouldn't see watery eyes. He couldn't put his hand over hers to comfort her. He couldn't do a thing in the middle of the messy scene.

It was one of those moments he wished his phone would ring and he'd be called to an emergency. Tony didn't move or say a word. He hated seeing anyone in a miserable situation, and it was clear this decision was very monumental for Laura. He wanted to make it better somehow, but he was afraid anything he said would only make things worse.

"If those noodles are so good your sister is thinking of moving here, I think we should definitely have them at our wedding," Kevin said.

Tony thought his cousin was taking a huge risk trying to inject humor at such a tense time, but Kevin knew Nicole. He'd won her over when she'd been dead set against falling in love with a firefighter. Love must have some strange magic, but it wasn't something Tony had experienced yet. He hadn't dated anyone he would have fought to win over. Maybe he needed to date more, but he hadn't found anyone who understood the demands of his career.

Laura would understand.

Tony took a deep breath and willed himself fifteen minutes into the future when he could escape the confines of the table and his own struggle to fight the feelings Laura evoked in him.

"I'm trying some," Kevin said, reaching across the table with his fork and scooping up several noodles from Laura's plate. He stuffed them in his mouth, rolled his eyes and groaned. "Amazing."

"You're ridiculous," Nicole said, a tiny smile breaking the tension on her face. She swiped at her eyes with her napkin. "And you're ridiculous, too," she said to Laura. "You can't keep your job here when summer ends. The beach gets really quiet in the fall and winter."

"I could do something else."

"Not firefighting," Nicole said.

Laura leaned back in her chair and put her napkin on the table. The last family dinner Tony had been involved in that was this tense was the night his eighteen-year-old sister announced she was pregnant while his mother served up meatloaf and carrots.

"There's plenty of summer left," Kevin said. "But only a few weeks until our wedding. So I'm going to vote for noodles and chicken breasts."

Everyone turned to look at him.

"Maybe a salad, too."

Tony was amazed that Kevin had managed to dispel the tension and stick with the task at hand. He was accustomed to bravery and leadership from all the men in his family, but he was impressed.

On the way out, after Tony insisted on leaving a generous tip even though their meals were complimentary, Kevin and Nicole stopped to talk with the restaurant's catering manager. Laura and Tony paused on the small patio outside the main entrance. There were benches and low lighting mixed with potted trees and plants. "Want to sit down?" Tony asked.

Laura shook her head. "I'm sorry I made that so uncomfortable."

"It's okay." Tony reached for her hand and gently squeezed it. It was a gesture he'd used many times, comforting someone at a fire scene or dealing with a serious illness. But the feel of Laura's hand in his reminded him that she wasn't just anyone. She glanced up at him with an open expression of vulnerability he hadn't seen since the previous summer, and he let her go.

"I've been trying to tell my sister how unhappy I was with my job," Laura said, "but she doesn't seem to think I'm serious. I don't know why not."

"Maybe it's because you seem so put together. She has a hard time picturing you doing something radical."

"I seem put together?"

"Yes." He wouldn't have thought so based on his brief interactions with Laura the previous summer, but from his first contact with her on the beach as she rescued those teens from the surf, Laura had impressed him with her determination. He just didn't know where her determination might lead her. "This year," he clarified with a grin.

"I'm a work-in-progress," she said.

"A good work."

Laura smiled, acknowledging a conversation they'd had weeks ago. "It means a lot to me that you think so, but you hardly know me, Tony."

"That's true, but—"

Kevin and Nicole came out of the restaurant and interrupted him, and he was very glad. He'd just been about to say *that's true, but I'd like to know you better.*

CHAPTER NINE

LAURA LIKED THE RAIN. She enjoyed watching it streak down the windows of her classroom on the days when she didn't have bus duty. She liked sitting by the window on a Saturday and reading one of the many historical novels that popped up as suggestions on her e-reader. She even liked going for a run in the rain, as long as it was a warm rain and she could find her old running shoes in the bottom of the closet.

Proving her strength and agility in the pouring rain while wearing turnout gear, a heavy helmet and clunky boots was not any fun. Not that she had signed on for fun.

"We didn't tell you much about tonight's activities because I didn't want you to get too worked up about it. This is practice, and we want you all to pass the test," Tony said. He stood just inside the open bay doors at the back of the station, the class of eight volunteers just inside. Rain fell in sheets behind Tony, and Laura thought he looked as if he were standing in front of a waterfall.

"I considered canceling the outdoor part of the agility training tonight, but I decided it might make an excellent point. We get called out in every kind of weather imaginable. Snow is a rarity, but ice has knocked us on our can more than once. You might think rain would extinguish a fire without our help, but you'd be surprised by how long a fire can rage inside a building before it breaks through."

Like people, Laura thought. She wondered what kind of fire was burning inside her fellow volunteers. A night like this one would test whatever was there. Most of the people in the class had developed a congenial relationship, leaning on each other in class and at the hands-on CPR training earlier in the week. They would need each other tonight, but Laura wondered if Allen would be willing to partner up and trust anyone. So far, he'd been a loner. She glanced over at him as he grimly listened to Tony. Maybe he had his reasons, but the firefighting world seemed to have a strong social component that Allen wasn't in tune with.

"You'll get a partner," Tony said. "And the two of you will race the clock to roll out hose, hook to the hydrant on the street behind the station and charge the line." Tony gestured to a red fire hydrant waiting for them. They'd learned all about hydraulics, water pressure and the importance of getting the hose rolled out and ready before giving the signal to open the water valve. Once charged, they had learned about several ways to control the end of the hose and direct the water.

But tonight they were going to try it in the pouring rain.

Gavin Kennedy and two other firefighters were suited in their gear to help with the training. Tony pointed to Oliver and Skip and paired them up. Then Marshall and Diane, Richard and Brock, and finally Laura and Allen.

Allen would have been her last choice only because she didn't know how to predict his behavior. Still, though he hadn't made any friends, he'd shown up to every class and paid attention with total intensity. Laura remembered the first night of class when he'd declared he wasn't afraid of anything.

"Which end do you want?" Allen asked, skipping a friendly greeting. "I can handle either one."

Of course you can. Laura smiled. "I can, too, so you go ahead and choose. Roll hose or hook and open the hydrant?"

They'd already been told that the person who stays on the hydrant end to hook up the hose and open the hydrant must then run the length of the hose their partner had rolled out. They both needed to have their hands on the nozzle at the end and direct the stream to hit an orange cone to complete the timed task. Both jobs were physically tough and demanded speed and strength.

"You do the hydrant. You know how, right?" he said.

In addition to reading and annotating the chapter in the book about couplers, valves and hydrants, Laura had also been in the front row when Tony demonstrated using the spanner wrench to unleash the water inside the hydrant. She had absorbed everything he said, fully aware that someone's life might one day depend on her knowledge.

It could be her own life, Tony's, her future brother-in-law's or anyone on the Cape Pursuit Fire Department.

"I know how," she said. She wanted to ask him if he knew how to roll out a reel of hose, but she didn't want to make an enemy of the man. He reminded her of one of the guys she had dated over the winter. An assistant football coach, Eric always wanted to prove himself to other men. Allen had that same hungry expression. Not a bad guy, but a guy who would benefit from more confidence in himself. "I know you'll do great at laying out the hose. You'll probably be the fastest one," she said.

A flicker of a smile passed over Allen's face, but it was quickly overcome by his grim determination. Fine; she'd tried.

Two teams lined up next to the hydrant and Gavin got ready to time them with the stopwatch app on his phone, which he sheltered under his fire helmet from the heavy rain. He'd already told them their times only mattered for bragging rights and they could learn a lot from the exercise no matter how they placed.

"Go!" Tony yelled.

Laura looped a section of hose around the hydrant to give herself some slack and prevent her partner from pulling it away from her. She attached her hose to the hydrant and waited, spanner wrench in hand, as she watched Allen roll the hose out straight and flat—well, mostly, except for an S-curve about halfway down. He gave her the signal that he was ready for water, and she assumed he was done laying the hose. She opened the valve on top of the hydrant, made sure the water started charging through the hose and took off running.

She was proud of being able to run despite the wet pavement, heavy clothes and awkward boots, and she chose a path right along the hose so she'd have the shortest route. No other teams had attempted the task yet, so she had no way to judge how fast she and Allen would compare. It certainly *seemed* as if they were kicking butt.

Laura was halfway down the length of fire hose when Allen suddenly grabbed and tugged the hose to try to pull out the curved section. Running fast right alongside the hose that had now moved, Laura's foot came down and rolled over the top of the rigid hose.

In one sickening moment, she knew she was going down. Too much speed and heavy gear combined with the element of surprise gave her no time to pivot or react. She tried controlling her fall, but she had to let go and let it happen, crashing headlong into the concrete and rolling twice. Her helmet came off and she heard a loud gasp from the spectators. She felt the entire thing as if she were in an action movie. When she landed on her back, she looked up into Tony's face. His eyes were wide, his hair streaked with rain, and he bent over her as if she were a glass vase that had smashed on the floor.

"Get me up," she said, holding up one gloved hand.

"No," he said. "Stay still. You may be hurt."

Laura did a quick review of her body parts and decided she had only one choice: finish the competition. She ignored Tony, rolled to her feet and got up. She grabbed her helmet, jammed it on her head and raced to the end of the line where Allen waited, stunned by her fall.

"I'm ready," she said. She grabbed the

nozzle, and Allen nodded at her and turned it on. Together they aimed it at the orange cone and knocked it over quickly with the force of their stream.

"Time," Gavin yelled. "And that was one heck of a show."

"Sorry," Laura said to Allen as he closed off the flow of water from the nozzle.

"My fault for moving the hose," he grunted. And then he looked at her with a small gleam of friendliness, water dripping off the edge of his helmet. "You got up."

Tony stalked up to Laura, his face red under the rivers of water.

"I always get up," she said to Allen.

"Not when I tell you not to," Tony said.

"Sorry." Laura shook her head. "Sometimes I get back up especially when people are least expecting it."

"Inside," he said. "I want to check you over and make sure you're not hurt."

"I'm fine," she said, holding out both arms and turning in a slow circle. "All my limbs are attached and working like they're supposed to."

"Go," he said, pointing toward the station. If it hadn't been pouring rain, Laura might have argued, but going inside was appealing. And, now that the adrenaline had abated, one of her elbows did feel as if someone had rubbed it with sandpaper and soaked it in rubbing alcohol.

As she trudged into the station where her classmates waited just out of the rain, Laura wondered if Tony planned to order her into the ambulance for a medical assessment. It was nice that he cared, and she couldn't get the image of his worried expression out of her mind. Of course, he cared for everyone under his command. She wasn't special. Was she?

"Diane," Tony said. "Will you help Laura out of that gear and make sure she's okay?"

"Sure," Diane said.

"I'm fine," Laura protested.

"We'll see," Tony said. He turned and walked back to the group, but he glanced over his shoulder as if to make sure Diane was following orders.

"Let's go in the break room," Diane said. "Not so many eyes there."

Laura left a puddle of water on the concrete floor. "Let me take this gear off here and leave it over a drain," she said. "I don't want to mess up the carpet in the break room." Diane helped her out of the coat and Laura stepped free of the bunker pants and boots. She felt twenty pounds lighter, but she was damp with rain and sweat. She clapped a hand over her elbow when the air hit it and bit her lip.

"I did the ambulance inspection last Sunday," Diane said as she inspected Laura's arm. "I know just where the first aid supplies are kept."

"It's no big deal, just a scrape."

"So we'll toss a bandage on it and you can get back in action," Diane said. She opened the side door of the ambulance and they both got in. Laura sat on the vinyl bench seat while Diane gathered an antiseptic wipe, some antibiotic cream and some gauze and wrap. "That's a nasty scrape."

"I can't even see how it happened under that heavy coat. You'd think you could jump off a bridge and survive with that gear."

"I wouldn't advise it," Diane said. "I couldn't believe you popped right back up after that spectacular wipeout."

"Experience," Laura said.

"You fall down a lot?"

"Not literally, but life seems to want to throw challenges my way, just to see what I'll do."

Diane put soothing ointment on Laura's elbow. "Is that why you're joining the department?"

"You mean, do I think being a first responder will help me stomp out my own fires?"

Diane laughed. "You could put it that way."

Laura took a deep breath and let it out slowly. "It's hard for me to put into words why I'm here. And you're probably going to think it's the worst possible place for me if I tell you."

"You don't have to tell me."

"It's okay. It's really no secret. Tony and Kevin both know, and a few of the others, I think." Laura gathered her courage for a moment, a preparation of sorts she always had to go through before she could say the words. It was easier than it had been, but she didn't think she'd ever be able to say the words lightly. "My younger brother, Adam, was killed fighting a forest fire. Two years ago. He was twenty-one and he wanted to..." Her voice faltered a moment but she bolstered it with a deep breath. "He wanted to help people."

"Oh, honey," Diane said. "That must have been terrible."

"It was. It still is."

"And that's why you want to do this? To honor his memory?"

"Yes and no," Laura said. "I've tried a lot of things to help me accept his loss. I threw myself into work, I tried drinking to forget, I dated some guys who were so wrong for me that they made my life seem somehow right." She sighed and fought tears. "And through it all, I blamed myself because he was my little brother, and I'm the one who encouraged him to join the summer fire brigade."

"It's not your fault."

"It feels like it." Laura smiled at Diane. "I've never even told my parents what I just told you, and they're going to panic when they find out what I'm doing."

"So what will you do now?"

"I'm done with running from my grief. I'm going to face it head on by doing something for other people. Not because Adam died, but so I can live."

Diane nodded and secured the gauze in place with a piece of tape. "When you feel helpless, help somebody."

"Exactly," Laura said. "And you know what? So far, I really like this. I like the trucks and the people and the knowing what to do in an emergency. I may even learn to walk in those boots without face-planting if I stick it out long enough."

"If you do, you'll have to share your secret with me. With my short legs, I don't think I'll ever be able to move gracefully in that gear, but nothing's going to stop me from trying," Diane said.

Laura heard a shoe on concrete just outside the ambulance door, and she expected to see Tony put his head in to check if she was alive despite her refusal to follow his orders. No one looked in on them, though, and she thought she must have heard wrong.

"We should get back out there," Laura said.

"You want to see if any of the other teams are beating your time, right?"

"If anyone does," Laura said, smiling at her friend, "I hope it's you."

TONY WANTED TO stand in the pouring rain and let it soak him all the way through, but people would wonder if he'd lost his mind.

Not because Adam died, but so I can live.

Laura's words to Diane had been private. Not meant for him or anyone else. He wondered if even her sister knew what drove Laura to become a firefighter. Her reason was raw and vivid, and quite possibly the best damn reason he'd ever heard for becoming a rescuer. Wanting to help other people so hard that you need it to live was both inexpressibly wonderful and terribly dangerous.

He'd thought Laura might be approaching the fire service with passion but a tender heart. It was even worse than that. Someone who believed so strongly in the work was bound to have her heart broken—perhaps irretrievably—the first time she failed to save someone. And it would happen. It had happened to all of them. What would such a fall do to Laura Wheeler?

"I hope you didn't start without me," Diane said to Marshall. "I'm ready to do this."

Marshall slung an arm around Diane. "Couldn't go without my partner. The two teams that tried it while you were patching up Laura didn't have any interesting mishaps, but their performance seemed to lack speed. Gavin is keeping the times a secret until we're all done."

"Excellent," Diane said. "As far as we know, we're playing for first place."

Tony grinned. Diane wasn't quite old enough to be his mother, but she was a role model for getting older without having hang-ups about it. He liked the way she was friendly to everyone and showed confidence without arrogance. She was a lot like Laura, and it was obvious that the two women had bonded.

He turned and looked into the station, wondering if Laura was going to suit up and come back out or if she was taking a break.

"How is Laura?" he asked Diane.

Diane pointed to Tony's other side where Laura stood in full turnout gear, just inside the station.

"I'm fine," Laura said. "A minor scrape but a grave injury to my pride. Running is supposed to be my superpower, but I don't think anyone is going to believe it after to-night."

"It wasn't your fault," Tony said, "Or anyone's. These things happen when you try to hurry."

"Then maybe you should have Gavin put away the stopwatch and we'll all amble through the exercise as if we have all the time in the world," Laura said, giving him a sideways grin from under the visor of her helmet.

Tony smiled and shook his head. "I think you're up, Diane."

While they watched the last team race the clock to charge the line and knock down the orange cone, Tony was highly aware of Laura standing next to him. The falling rain made a curtain through which they could see Diane and Marshall working together. The other five members of the group stood on the other side of Laura. When she had fallen, he wasn't the only person to rush out in the rain to try to help her.

All six spectators from her class had run to help, and Tony wondered if they had all feared the worst, as he had. It was a terrible fall, but Laura had taken it completely in stride. He'd heard what she told Diane about life giving her challenges.

"We have to find her shorter pants and boots that fit better," Laura said as she watched Diane roll out the length of hose.

"We?" Tony asked.

"I mean you." She pointed around at the

group. "Us, you know, everyone. The department."

"I know," Tony said. "When volunteers finish their training and decide for certain on a commitment, we invest in gear for them. It's expensive, so we prefer to share gear only when we're sure."

It would have been the perfect opportunity to ask her if she intended to stay in Cape Pursuit and become a full-time volunteer, but he couldn't open that conversation with other people around. He'd been stunned at the restaurant, and he wondered if Nicole's negative reaction and the potential displeasure of her parents might derail her decision to stay longer than the summer.

Tony turned his attention back to the physical drill. Marshall had the hydrant on, the water was quickly charging the line and he was racing to the other end where Diane waited with the nozzle already aimed at the orange cone.

"I think he's going to beat my time if he stays on his feet," Laura said. "Not that I'm surprised."

"You can try again another time. This

was just practice with the added challenge of weather."

"Only a few weeks left of training," Laura said. "And a few weeks until my sister's wedding. Have the guys gone to get measured for their suits yet?"

Tony nodded. "A few days ago. I went with Kevin and Tyler and their dad."

"Like a Ruggles family reunion," Laura commented.

"Seems like every day is a Ruggles family affair around here. But we don't usually dress up."

Although his dad had recently retired from the chief's spot, there were still often at least three members of his family at the station. The firefighters were like a family to him in other ways, too, and standing there chatting with Laura as they watched Diane and Marshall high-fiving each other in the pouring rain reminded him of how close a connection they had. Her sister was marrying his cousin who was like a brother to him. They would almost be related. It was one more reason why he needed to keep his relationship with Laura strictly professional.

Maybe if he thought of her as a sister or

cousin it would help, but he struggled to see her that way. Her smile, bravery and fleeting flashes of vulnerability made him want to take her in his arms and protect her from life, from everything. Yet that was the last thing she needed. Laura didn't want to exist in a velvet-lined version of the world. She wanted to face it. Was she testing herself?

If so, she had come to the right place.

"I wish I had taken pictures of this," Laura said. "It would be fun for all of us to remember how we started. When we're up there on the firefighters' hall of fame, we might forget what it felt like to be beginners," she added, laughing.

"I remember everything," Tony said. "Especially the firsts." He didn't want to tell her how vividly he recalled the first time he had failed, faced death without being able to do anything about it and grieved behind closed doors when the trucks were all washed and parked in the station.

"Well, I'd like to think of my performance tonight as a last and not a first," Laura said. "But I have a feeling this won't be the last time I'll have a spectacular crash."

Tony wished he could suggest another way

for Laura to feel alive and of service. Wanting to protect her was going to kill him.

"Which is why I think we ought to dig through your storage for some smaller boots sooner rather than later," she added, and then she turned and joined her classmates for a group high five.

Gavin snapped a picture with his phone, and Tony hoped he could think of a way to ask Gavin to text him that photo with eight joyful faces streaked with rain. As the class of volunteers laughed and congratulated each other, all Tony could see was the happiness on Laura's face. He wanted to hold on to that moment.

CHAPTER TEN

A FAN OF playing out scenarios in his head before they happened, Tony had already considered what he would do if a serious fire call came in while he was teaching the volunteer class.

So, in the middle of a lesson in the training room, when dispatch called and said flames were showing through the roof of a factory on the edge of town, Tony was ready. He had to go, and Gavin Kennedy did, too. Judging from the severity of the call, it would be all hands on deck.

"Work together and study chapter nine," Tony said, closing his book and heading for the door of the training room. "We could be gone for hours, so you can go home when you're done."

"Can we come along?" Skip asked. "We can help."

"Not without gear and certification. You

can stay put and listen to the radio traffic, and if we get back and you're still here, we'll be glad to have your help cleaning gear and washing the trucks."

As he spoke, Tony was leaving the room and heading for his own fire gear. He glanced back at the eight eager faces in the training room and hoped none of them would decide this was the night they would become a hero.

He jumped in the driver's seat of the first pumper, the one that would serve as both fire attack and incident command. In his twelve years on the department, Tony had seen his share of large fires, and it was something they continued to practice and plan for. He was still a mile away from the factory when he realized the dispatcher had not been ex- aggerating. The faded sunset in the west left enough darkness for him to see a faint or- ange glow where there shouldn't have been one.

"Smoke," Gavin said from the passenger seat. "Going to be a hot one."

"Call in the volunteers and Virginia Beach and put them on standby for mutual aid," Tony said.

Gavin got the dispatcher on the radio and did as Tony asked.

"Car on your right up there," Gavin said, pointing out a car that wasn't following the protocol of pulling off to the right when an emergency vehicle was behind it. He pulled the air horn and the car dove into a driveway.

"I think you scared him off his phone," Tony said.

"Good. I hate tourists on phones."

"Someday that could be you. Lost on vacation with crying kids in the back seat," Tony said. "You should show pity."

Gavin laughed and then swore softly. "Those flames. Man. What kinds of hazards are we looking at in the factory?"

"All of them," Tony said.

"They build boats, right?"

Tony nodded.

"So, wood, fiberglass, paint, varnish, glue, vinyl, foam," Gavin listed. "Basically every toxic thing known to man that can burn."

"We'll need a decent perimeter. Keep people back."

Tony got on the radio, identified himself and reminded all his men about getting into their full gear, including air packs, because of the hazardous fumes. He told them no one was going anywhere near the burning structure until he gave a direct order.

"The roof's already gone," he commented to Gavin when he got off the radio.

"Surround and drown?" Gavin asked.

"May be the only thing we can do," Tony said. "We'll have to see if the fire walls within the plant have done anything. Maybe we can save parts of the building if we get behind the fire and drive it out, but I'm not putting anyone at risk of a falling roof unless we have reports of people entrapped."

"Parking lot looks empty," Gavin said as soon as they got close enough to visualize an entire wall of the factory and feel the heat through the open windows of the fire truck. "No second shift working. Must be how the fire got such a head start."

"I wish I had ten more trucks and twenty more men," Tony said. "Luckily, we've got good hydrants on this side of town and the owners worked with the city to install more when they built this place."

Tony pulled up next to a hydrant and parked where his truck would serve as incident command. He grabbed a portable radio and directed his incoming trucks where to park and how to set up. He'd need water supply, lights and plenty of hose. The ladder truck, driven by Kevin and Tyler, rumbled down the driveway, its engine and weight giving it a unique sound Tony would know anywhere, even over the roar of flames and sirens.

There was nothing like having a solid team of people who were practically family when facing a heart-pounding emergency. His thoughts flashed to the new recruits back at the station. Maybe he should have let them ride along on one of the trucks, but he couldn't risk their lives when he didn't have time to think about ensuring their safety on top of the rest of the department.

They would have their chance.

Tony didn't measure time passing, but he noticed the increasing darkness and deep shadows being thrown by the tower lights from his rescue truck. The owners of the factory had shown up not long after the outriggers went down on the ladder truck, and they had confirmed that the factory would be empty. The first shift had gone home hours ago, and there were only two cars in the employee lot—both of the car owners were accounted for, and were after-hours maintenance who had discovered and called in the fire. They'd been working in a different part of the building and the flames were beyond their ability to use fire extinguishers on.

With no victims entrapped, Tony had been able to immediately shift his attack plan to containment. Keeping the fire out of the parts of the so-far unaffected building and keeping the flames from leaping to other buildings on the property was hard enough.

The local newspaper showed up, the reporter snapping pictures and asking questions. Tony saw him on the periphery of the fire scene, talking with bystanders. He wanted to delegate someone to keep people back and set up tape, but all his firefighters and the volunteers they'd called in were busy knocking down flames and supplying water. The police usually showed up in full force and helped, but Tony heard the radio traffic, and he knew they had their hands full. They were busy with a domestic violence standoff on the other side of town. When one lone police car showed up to close off the side streets leading to the fire scene, he was grateful for the only help the Cape Pursuit Police were able to offer.

As Tony glanced at the edge of the fire scene, he saw several personal vehicles park on the edge of the factory's long driveway. Doors opened and eight people poured out. The class of volunteers. And the person at the front of the pack was a tall, slender woman whose silhouette he recognized even as it was splashed with red and white from the flashing lights.

He clenched his jaw; his first reaction was frustration that they had not done as he asked and stayed in the station, studying chapter nine in their books. He watched the group stop when Laura held up her hand just on the edge of the fire scene. Tony waited a moment, wondering what they would do now that they were here. He was tempted to stalk over there and serve them up a lecture, but two things stopped him. He remembered his own training and eagerness. In their shoes, would he have sat in the training room and waited?

And he couldn't deny that he needed their help. His full-time firefighters and volunteers were busy. Crowds were gathering, watching the flames, taking pictures and videos with their phones. If someone slipped between the trucks and got closer to the fire scene, they would be in trouble.

He grabbed Gavin as he laid down a ladder next to the rescue truck. "Go over there," Tony said, pointing at the eight volunteers, "and tell our class to grab reflective vests from the rescue truck and spread out. They can keep bystanders back."

"Can't believe they showed up," Gavin said. "That was brave but a little stupid."

Gavin's assessment of the volunteers' action as stupid raised Tony's opinion of the young firefighter a notch. The kid was right, but there would be time to address that later. Right now, he could use their help.

"Tell them what I said," Tony said. "Laura knows where the vests are."

LAURA SAW TONY'S face in the harsh light of the fire scene. Lights from the tops of the trucks bounced off the reflective stripes on Tony's gear, but his expression was clear. He wasn't happy to see them. She'd known she was taking a chance when she suggested to her classmates that they could at least drive over to the fire scene and observe it.

They had already discussed the assigned chapter in the book, despite keeping one ear on the radio traffic. As they sat in the training room, she noticed how fidgety her classmates were. A shaking leg, a bouncing pen on a notebook. What if the firefighters needed more help? She'd heard the call over the radio to put Virginia Beach's department on standby, but she hadn't heard any more talk.

"No entrapment," a voice had said over the radio. "Building empty." It was Tony's voice, and Laura caught the subtle notes of relief mixed with tension in the four words.

There had to be a way they could help.

"I'm off duty," Marshall said, "but the police department has its hands full with that domestic standoff. They may not have extra units available to direct traffic away from the fire scene."

"So, should we go and do that?" Laura asked.

The eight classmates had exchanged tense glances.

"Group decision," Laura said, "but I say we go."

And now that they were on the edge of the lighted circle, what were they going to do? Laura saw Gavin approaching and expected him to deliver a lecture from the chief and probably tell them to go away.

"Chief says get reflective vests from the rescue truck and spread out on the edges. Keep people back. May be some hazardous fumes, but wind's going the other way, so you'll be okay on this side."

Relief flooded Laura's mind. Tony wasn't mad?

"Chief says you know where the vests are on the truck," Gavin said to Laura. "Keep people back, don't talk to the media."

"Not the worst job," Marshall said. "Feels a bit like my day job. Show me where the vests are and I'll help you hand them out."

Laura went straight to the outside compartment on the driver's side where she remembered road safety equipment being stored. Vests, road flares, even a reflective sign warning drivers of danger ahead. She dug out a stack of vests and handed them to Marshall, keeping one for herself.

"Should we spread out or work in pairs?" she asked Marshall. "This is your area of expertise."

He looked around. "I think we have to spread out or we won't be able to cover the wide circle around this place."

Laura nodded. The boat building factory seemed gigantic. They put on their vests and spread out on the side of the factory Gavin had indicated, upwind of potential fumes. Laura hoped there was no one on the other side; Marshall had said it wasn't likely because there were no streets or sidewalks that could access it. It backed up to an industrial park that was mostly empty.

She faced the groups of curious onlookers, away from the fire. When any bystanders got too close, she advised them politely to step back for their own safety. Although she would rather have grabbed a fire hose and helped knock down the flames, she was already risking Tony's good opinion just by showing up. But it had to be a good sign that he hadn't sent them home, right?

After a half hour, she saw a vehicle she recognized. Her sister. Nicole and her friend Jane got out of the car and opened the back hatch. Laura knew what they were doing. Jane's husband, Charlie, was on the department, but long before she had married him, she had faithfully shown up at fire scenes with food and coffee.

Laura waved at her sister and Jane, but she stood her ground. She wanted to go help lug coffee and food to the firefighters, but she wasn't a girlfriend, a wife or even a concerned citizen. She was—sort of—one of them, and she had taken up a post on the perimeter and couldn't relinquish it. Tony was counting on her class of volunteers, whether he'd wanted them there or not.

She heard a crash and a shout and whipped around just in time to see part of the roof collapse. She knew from radio traffic and observation on scene that Tony had not allowed anyone to go into the burning part of the building. Thank goodness. There was a man on the end of the ladder extending from the truck way over the building. He directed a heavy stream of water down into the burned structure, but he was out of harm's way.

Was it Kevin?

Laura looked back at Nicole, wondering how she would react to seeing such a dangerous aspect of her fiancé's job—a job that had taken her months to accept, even though and because she loved him. Nicole watched the man on the end of the long ladder, hanging over the flames. Laura guessed her sister knew who it was. And then Nicole turned her troubled gaze on Laura. She looked as if she was going to cry, and Laura felt sick and miserable. Was she behaving selfishly, embracing the career that had killed their brother as a way for her own heart to heal?

Her eyes locked with her sister's for a moment, and Laura was immensely relieved that Nicole hadn't shed a tear. Instead, she squared her shoulders and marched behind Jane to the main pumper where Tony stood guard, talking on his radio.

Jane and Nicole put a big thermos and a stack of cups on the running board and set a box next to it. Laura guessed from experience that there were sandwiches in that box, enough for every firefighter on scene to have one or two. Would they be there all night? Jane and Nicole only talked to Tony for a minute and then Jane went back to her car and Nicole came over to Laura.

"Jane's baby is asleep in her car seat," Nicole

said. "We can't stay, but if you're going to be here half the night, call me and I'll bring more food and coffee."

"Okay," Laura said. She forced a smile, even though her sister's expression was grim. "Thank you."

"You could volunteer at the humane society," Nicole said. "Puppies and kittens give unconditional love. I was thinking about this after our dinner last week when we were talking about how we used to bring home animals."

Laura waited out her sister, knowing there was nothing she could say.

"You love animals," Nicole said. "You're really smart. I bet you could be a vet. It's sort of like firefighting. There are animal emergencies all the time."

"I'll see you when I get home," Laura said.

Nicole sighed. "I don't know if I should go to Kevin's house and wait up for him or stay at our house and wait up for you. You two are determined to kill me."

"You could go home with Jane and wait together. I'll call you when we're done," Laura said.

Nicole gave Laura a quick hug. "No matter

what time," Nicole said, and then she turned and fled toward Jane's car without looking back.

Hours later when the fire was completely defeated, Laura and her classmates helped roll up hose and pack equipment back on the trucks. One truck and two firefighters stayed on scene in case of flare-ups, but the rest of the department returned to the station. Adrenaline gone, Laura wondered what Tony would say to her and the other new volunteers. They'd been helpful, but they'd also disobeyed his specific orders.

It was two o'clock in the morning, and deep weariness caught up with her as she helped wash and replace equipment. She had to open the Pursuit of Fun beach shack in only six hours, but she wasn't complaining. When she signed up to volunteer, she knew there would be late nights, early mornings and everything in between.

"Go home," Tony said, surprising her by appearing behind her as she folded the vests she and her fellow volunteers had worn. "It's late, or early, however you want to look at it."

"Are you going home?" she asked.

"No. I'm going to stay and write up the

reports. Insurance company and state fire inspector will be here in the morning, so I'll stick around."

Laura finished stowing the vests and closed the cabinet on the side of the rescue truck. Grime streaked Tony's face, and she wanted to reach up and wipe it off.

"It was your idea, wasn't it?" he asked. "Coming to the fire, even though I told you not to."

Laura never considered lying. She knew the risk she had taken, and she was willing to own it.

"Yes. I couldn't stand just waiting around. It seemed as if there was something we could do."

Tony didn't answer; he just stared at her as if there was something he wanted to say.

"We finished the chapter you assigned. Took notes and everything. And then Marshall heard that most of the police department was tied up on the other side of the city, and he told us what role the police usually play at fire scenes." She was trying not to ramble or take a defensive tone. Just stating the facts and giving Tony a replay of what led to her decision. "I asked for a group decision, and in the end we decided we'd all go."

Tony swiped a hand across his forehead and left a wider streak of dirt. "I know you were trying to be a leader, but you have to learn that being a leader sometimes means not jumping in with both feet."

She was too tired to argue and she knew nothing good would come of it. But didn't she have the right to defend her actions? "Would you rather we didn't show up and keep bystanders back?" she asked.

"Everyone's safety is my responsibility," he said.

"And?" He hadn't answered her question.

"And we'll talk about this as a group at our next meeting," he said. "You go home. The rest of the volunteers have left."

She was being dismissed. Politely and mercifully before she said more than she should. She didn't want to argue with Tony, but she did want something from him. His approval, yes, but something more than that.

His friendship.

He wasn't like a lot of the men she knew back home. The male teachers at her high school had emotional fortitude, the willingness to keep trying with adolescents in the classroom and on the field. A few guys she had dated were mostly interested in themselves. But Tony had physical and emotional bravery, and she highly doubted he got up every day wondering how he could improve his own situation in life.

She admired him, liked him. But that was as far as her feelings could possibly go.

She turned and walked away and was almost to the big overhead doors still open to the night air when she heard him say her name quietly.

"Your heart was in the right place," he said.

She'd be able to go to sleep with those words quieting her mind.

CHAPTER ELEVEN

SUMMERS IN CAPE PURSUIT were hot, and even though Laura loved to run, the heat discouraged her from putting in miles unless she got out very early or very late. On the summer solstice, the longest day of the year, Laura helped register runners for the Cape Pursuit Fire Department 5K. Held downtown at a tourist location, the goal was to raise money for the department and raise awareness of the need to check smoke-detector batteries twice a year.

She'd already convinced her fellow volunteers to attend the event, and some of them even to run it. Marshall said he was a decent runner and, to her surprise, Allen also said he enjoyed running. It was the first personal thing she'd learned about him. Laura imagined Allen probably wished he'd taken the running portion of their exercise in the rain the night Laura had fallen on her face.

But then she would have missed out on the chance to humiliate herself for the cause.

She would never forget Tony's face as he looked down at her, obviously fearing she'd maimed herself.

"I never thought I'd own a jogging stroller," Jane said as she dropped off brochures about city events to be handed out at the registration table. "Much less push one in a race. But I feel obligated as a member of the city council and the fire department family, so here I am sweating it out like a good mom."

"You're a great mom. Tell you what, if it's close at the end, I'll let you beat me," Laura offered. "That will make you feel better."

Jane laughed. "No way is it going to be close."

Laura cocked her head. "Don't be too sure. I've decided to join the firefighters who run in full turnout gear. Boots, bunker pants, helmet, everything. So I'm not going to break any speed records, and I'll be lucky to finish."

"You'll die in this heat."

"Gloriously," Laura said. "Like a hero."

"A hero would push my jogging stroller for me."

"Get Charlie to do it. Tell him it's the price of fatherhood."

"He'll be at the station tonight," Jane said. "So he won't even be able to see my triumph with the baby buggy. I think he volunteered to be on call just to avoid stroller duty."

"He's not that shallow. I'm sure he's making a sacrifice for the greater good," Laura said.

Jane's baby started fussing, and Jane grinned apologetically at Laura and started pushing the buggy around the downtown parking lot where the race would begin and end. Runners were already hanging around, fastening on their race bibs and warming up with short jogs up and down the street.

A cool ocean breeze blew away some of the day's heat, but Laura still worried she'd wilt over the course of three point one miles. She wasn't going to embarrass herself, especially dressed in CPFD gear, so she would tough it out. Kevin would be running, as well as Gavin, Ethan and Travis. And, of course, Tony.

Laura picked up a small bottle of sports

drink and downed it, hydrating her cells and willing them not to let her down. The other people helping at the registration table were all wives of full-time firefighters or volunteers. Laura wore her favorite black running shorts and a sleeveless top emblazoned with the name of the high school where she worked.

Used to work. She still had a few weeks, but her time in Cape Pursuit was teaching her something she hadn't learned in four years on the faculty. She didn't want to be in Indiana where winter lasted forever and she measured time by which American history posters she put up in her classroom. She couldn't face going back there.

"Either you're mad, or that's your game face and you're plotting a way to smoke the competition," Tony said. "Should I be worried?"

Laura laughed. "Neither one. I was thinking about my classroom."

Tony raised both eyebrows but didn't say anything.

"And how I was dreading the thought of eventually tacking up the Civil War poster showing the major battles and then moving on to the inventions of the Industrial Revolution."

"I liked that part of history," Tony said. Instead of his navy blue pants, Tony wore shorts with a fire department T-shirt. He looked more approachable than he usually did at the station. "The fire service really became important during the age of manufacturing. I should have you teach a class on the history of fire brigades in America."

"Only if there's no test at the end and I don't have to sign any hall passes."

"Deal," Tony said. "I found you some gear I hope will work. It's in the truck."

He pointed to the pumper he'd driven over from the station and parked prominently at the entrance to the parking lot where the race would start.

"Does it have a built-in air conditioner?"

"No, but it's close to fitting you. Belonged to a guy who used to be on our department."

"What happened to him?" Laura asked.

"Moved on to the big city department in Norfolk. Happens once in a while that we're a stepping stone to the big departments, but most people are happy to stay here," Tony said.

"Like you and your family."

He shrugged. "This is our home. Come try on your gear. I'll put mine on, too, and we'll drum up pledges and support for the burn unit at the hospital. People are generous, especially if we're willing to run three miles in bunker gear."

Laura followed Tony over to the truck and stepped into the pants and boots he set out for her. He was right; it was much closer to her size. She could almost picture herself surviving the race, even though she knew she was risking saucer-sized blisters on her feet by running in boots. Tony held her coat while she slid her arms into it, and he hiked it around her shoulders. His fingers grazed her neck and she felt very warm.

"Decent fit?" he asked.

Laura nodded, and Tony handed her a helmet. She gathered her hair into a low ponytail at the base of her neck so it wouldn't interfere and then she strapped on the helmet.

"Looks good," he said.

Laura almost said thank you, but she realized he must be talking about the safe fit of the helmet instead of offering any compliment on her appearance. Tony slipped off his street shoes and put on his bunker pants and boots. Laura considered helping him with his coat, but he had it on and buckled so fast she didn't have time. *Experience*.

"Have you run in gear before?" she asked.

"Every year since I've been on the department. This year is hotter than usual, so I hope I don't ruin my record of finishing in a decent spot. As long as I beat at least one other guy on the department, I can live with myself."

"Does that include me?"

Tony laughed. "I don't expect to beat you to the finish line unless Allen shows up and trips you with a hose."

"Not proud of that," Laura said.

Tony's smile faded. "I was just glad you were okay." He swallowed and looked away, then turned his helmet over and adjusted the straps on the inside. "I'd hate to lose a good volunteer."

"I keep waiting for you to say something about the fire at the boat factory," Laura said, blurting out the thing that had been weighing on her mind for days. "About me, us, disobeying your direct orders."

He put his helmet on. "I'd rather you'd

stayed at the station, but I can't deny you were helpful. The only thing is, I...found it distracting."

"But I thought we were helping get rid of distractions, keeping bystanders from creeping too close or reporters from asking questions."

"You did. But I kept looking in your direction to make sure you were okay." He met her eyes. "I mean all of you, all the volunteers. You're my responsibility."

"We were well away from the fire, out of harm's way."

He shook his head. "You never know. Things happen." He handed her an empty boot with a laminated sign pinned to the side. There was a picture of a red-faced firefighter running in gear with sweat flying off him and a note asking for donations for the burn unit. "Let's get some cash. If we're going to suffer during this race, we might as well make it worthwhile."

Laura fell into step beside Tony and she was glad he did all the talking to spectators waiting for the race to start as she held the boot and collected money. It gave her time to think about what he'd said—about watching her to see if she was okay. Although he'd immediately clarified that he meant everyone, his expression and tone made her wonder if he felt something between them that was more than the relationship he had with the other firefighters.

It shouldn't be. And it couldn't be good. Laura was not going to be a walking cliché and fall for a man in uniform who also happened to be her boss. She and Diane would be the first female members of the Cape Pursuit Fire Department, and she wasn't going to mess that up by doing something embarrassing. Tony was a respected firefighter and leader. She could learn a lot from him.

More importantly, everything she learned about responding to emergencies and taking control of a situation that could be possibly out of control put her closer to realizing her own potential and happiness.

TONY LINED UP at the front of the pack with five other firefighters in full gear. He told them all to pace themselves and not try to be heroes, but he knew darn well they would all compete with themselves and each other.

He'd run with three of them before, but Marshall and Laura were wild cards.

It was past sunset, but it wasn't dark. The evening light would last another hour, and all the runners had glow sticks, necklaces and bracelets. It added a layer of safety and fun. The firefighters running in gear already had reflective stripes, and he noticed Laura had attached a glow stick to her helmet, anyway.

One of the police officers fired a starter's pistol, and the dozens of runners took off. Athletes in shorts and sneakers quickly overtook Tony's group, but he didn't let it bother him. Instead he focused on the sizable donation for the burn unit. That was what mattered.

As long as he wasn't the last firefighter across the finish line.

He passed familiar local businesses in downtown Cape Pursuit. They all had their lights on and lanterns out front for the summer solstice event. Bystanders clapped for all the runners, but especially for the firefighters running in full gear. Marshall dropped back after the first mile, but Laura kept pace with the group. Tony glanced over several times and noticed her flushed face in the streetlights they passed. She took off her helmet once and swiped back stray hairs.

As they approached the two-mile marker, Tony felt as if he were standing unsheltered in front of a raging inferno. He remembered the incredible heat from his previous nine runs, and he vividly recalled nearly passing out once and being tempted to strip off his coat or quit three other times. He slowed his pace to accommodate the heat. Took a cup of water from a race volunteer and noticed Laura did the same.

One more mile. He could do it. A runner Tony had known since high school dropped back, pressing a hand to his side, so Tony ran alongside him and talked for a few minutes. When the man stopped at a water station and waved Tony on, Tony noticed that Laura was no longer next to him.

Had she dropped back without his noticing? Been overcome by the heat? He turned and looked behind him, encumbered by his helmet and the darkness. He saw reflective turnout gear on the ground, a glow stick lodged in a helmet, also on the ground.

Tony stopped, pivoted and ran back. Was Laura okay? His heart burned in his chest and he thought he would burst into flames as he raced toward the firefighter on the ground. When he reached her, he realized immediately that the problem wasn't with Laura. She was helping a woman who sat on the ground clutching her lower leg.

"Charley horse," Laura said. She massaged the woman's leg. "Used to see it all the time with the kids on the cross-country team."

Tony dropped to his knees beside Laura and immediately felt his own leg seize up. He gritted his teeth.

"Are you okay?" he asked.

"Just hot," the woman said, "I shouldn't have bypassed the water station, but I was trying to place in my age category. Some of these women in the forty to forty-five group are monsters." She flopped back on the ground.

Laura laughed. "Maybe their legs will be so sore tomorrow they'll have to go backward down steps."

"That makes me feel better," the woman on the ground said. "I'm going to picture that as I limp across the finish line."

A race volunteer dashed over with two

cups of water and Laura made the woman drink an entire one while she continued to rub out the cramp.

"Ready to get up?" Laura asked, and the woman nodded in agreement. Laura gave Tony a strange look, probably surprised he wasn't being more helpful, but he was trying to keep a neutral expression on his face despite the murderous cramp in his own leg.

Laura handed him the other cup of water. "You drink this," she said.

She stood and helped the other woman up, steadying her for a moment and then watching her take off with an awkward gait to rejoin the race. Laura held out a hand to Tony, but he shook his head. "Need a minute." He downed the cup of water and tried to imagine it reaching all the overheated parts of his body and rejuvenating them.

"You have leg cramps, too?"

He nodded. "The mother of all leg cramps. I stopped suddenly and squatted, and now I'm probably going to lose the leg. You can leave me here for dead."

Laura laughed. "You won't die."

"Okay, Chief?" Marshall asked as he jogged by.

Tony groaned.

Jane race-walked past with her jogging stroller. "Need a lift?" she asked.

"Get me up," Tony said, holding out a hand to Laura. "I'm begging you."

Laura pulled his arm across her shoulders and helped him to his feet. They took a few steps forward together, and bystanders burst into applause.

"My finest hour," Tony muttered. He broke into a painful slow jog, and Laura kept pace alongside him.

"You don't have to run to the finish line. In this heat, no one will judge you if you walk. You could talk to bystanders and remind them all to check the batteries in their smoke detectors. It would be a public service."

"Only a half mile to go," he said through gritted teeth.

Laura jogged next to him, though Tony suspected she could have left him behind. The pain in his leg eased, and running became easier as the bright lights at the finish line came into view. With only twenty feet to go, Laura said, "Do you want me to throw the race so you can beat me and pre-serve your pride?"

"No way," Tony said. He couldn't believe she had asked, and he wasn't going to take advantage of her kindness or his position as her commanding officer. "You deserve to beat me."

Their steps synced up, and they ran the last ten steps in unison. When they crossed the mat, Tony could not have said which of them was first.

CHAPTER TWELVE

"RIDE HOME?" NICOLE offered as she caught up with Laura after the race. Laura had shared a ride with her sister on the way to the race because Nicole had also volunteered to help organize the registrations, race start, food and awards. Laura's muscles were tired, but she was emotionally wide-awake from the exhilaration of the nighttime 5K and the sports drinks and bagel afterward.

Laura shivered in the night air now that she had taken off her heavy gear and stowed it back on the fire truck. Her running clothes underneath were damp, and her hair stuck to her neck.

"Thanks, but I'm going to stick around and finish the cleanup. I'll get a ride or walk home. It would probably do me some good to walk after sweating it out in that gear."

"I'll make sure she gets a ride home," Tony said. He had a folded table under one arm and two chairs under the other. "Several of us are sticking around."

"Are you sure?" Nicole asked.

"You have an early morning at the gallery," Laura said. "I'll be fine."

After Nicole left, Laura helped Tony gather up the leftover supplies, many of which they would reuse next year. Would she be here next year, volunteering on the fire department and working a local job? The race through the lighted streets of the town with locals and tourists cheering reminded her what a fun place Cape Pursuit was to live and how much her home on the outskirts of Indianapolis paled in comparison.

She helped Tony lower the pop-up tent and fold it into its carrying case. Together they hauled it across the parking lot and hoisted it into the back of his pickup truck. Their arms brushed as they pushed it into the bed and closed the tailgate, and Laura shivered, gooseflesh popping up on her skin. Wordlessly, Tony grabbed a sweatshirt from the front seat of his truck and handed it to Laura.

"Now that we're not running anymore, you feel the night air," he said, putting a light hand on her upper arm. "You'll get cold."

"Won't you be cold?" she asked. They stood close together, Tony's touch taking away the night's chill. With one step, she could be in his arms, but that was impossible. Maybe she was interpreting everything wrong and he felt nothing more for her than he did any of the other firefighters. She was not going to make a fool of herself.

Tony shook his head. She accepted the sweatshirt, a navy blue one with the insignia of the Cape Pursuit Fire Department on it, and pulled it on. It was lightweight, just right and obviously Tony's personal property. It smelled like him—a mixture of fire station and aftershave.

Tony's radio squawked and he held it up, listening. He turned and gestured to the other three firefighters who were still left. "Ambulance call. You two take it," he said to Ethan and Kevin, and then he pointed to Gavin, "and you take the pumper back to the station. I put the extra bottled water, bagels and bananas in the cab. Will you put them in the break room?"

Kevin and Ethan jumped in the ambulance and took off, and Gavin fired up the pumper.

"You're not going?" Laura asked.

"No, I don't go on every run unless it seems like it could get ugly. This was a call from the front desk at one of the hotels and it sounded like a precaution more than an emergency."

"So you're off duty and you can go home and have a hot shower," Laura said. She was already thinking about how good that would feel when she got back to the home she shared with her sister. She'd run in dozens of races ranging from a few miles to full marathons, and there was nothing like standing in a steaming shower for a long time afterward.

"I never feel like I'm off duty," Tony said. "But I don't take my radio into the shower with me."

Because she was wearing his sweatshirt, Laura could guess what his soap smelled like. It was personal, putting on someone else's clothing. She felt as if she was crossing a line, but Tony was a nice guy. He would lend a sweatshirt to anyone.

"Thanks for not smoking me at the finish line," he said.

Laura laughed. "My legs were too heavy to smoke anyone, even if I'd wanted to."

Tony leaned against the side of his pickup truck. They were alone in the parking lot.

"When I was in high school, I hated running," Tony said. "I was on the baseball team and didn't mind lifting weights and going to practice. But the running during conditioning was terrible."

"You like it now?"

He nodded. "I've matured. When I was seventeen, I just ran flat out as fast as I could no matter how far I had to go. Just tried to get from point A to point B. Once I discovered the magic of pacing myself, it changed my life."

"A good running coach would have told you that. That's the first lesson for my team. Next year's team has probably already met up with the head coach for summer training runs, and I'm sure they've heard it over and over. Pace yourselves. Sometimes slow and steady really do win the race."

"You're missing out on those training runs," Tony said. "Does that mean you won't be coaching the team, even if you do go back?"

Laura looked down. She began to feel the weight and lateness of the evening. Was Tony trying to make her doubt the wisdom of staying in Cape Pursuit? Did he wish she would go home and make things a lot simpler, a graceful exit from whatever was developing between them?

"Sorry," he said, before she had a chance to think of a way to answer him without sounding defensive or angry. She wasn't angry, just tired of people thinking they had the magical secret to how she could be the happy and productive person she deserved to be.

"I know you said you might not go back to teaching," he continued. "It's just that I've noticed—"

"What?" she asked, afraid he was going to say she wasn't cut out for the fire service and maybe she should go back to teaching, no matter how empty it left her.

"I've noticed how good you are with other people. You're patient, intuitive and explain things well. The class average on the volunteer test will probably set a record, and it won't be because of my instruction."

"Thanks," she said quietly. She appreciated his praise, but she also worried he'd said it to cover up something else he wanted to tell her. Did everyone think she should give up her plan to fight fires? Of all people, Tony should have understood her passion for wanting to serve. Wasn't that why he was there?

"If you weren't a fire chief," she asked, "what would you be doing?"

"No idea," he said. "Never thought about it."

"That's not a fair answer," she said. "We always have choices. There must have been a time when you made the conscious decision to make this your life's work."

Tony didn't answer, but Laura saw a serious expression cross his face, despite the low lighting in the parking lot.

"Have you ever doubted your decision?" she asked. It would make her feel so much better if he had. He couldn't always be the perfectly composed public servant he appeared to be. Where were the flaws and vulnerabilities that would make him human and make her feel better?

"I should take you home," Tony said.

"I don't mind walking."

Tony opened the passenger door of his truck and held it open. "I would mind if you walked home this late."

"What's going to happen in peaceful Cape Pursuit?"

"Anything can happen," Tony said. A smile broke his grim expression. "You have to pass by three miniature golf courses on your way home, and you could get sucked into an epic tournament that ends at dawn and makes you late to work. Or you could get a killer leg cramp, lie down on a park bench and get arrested for vagrancy."

Laura laughed and got in the truck. "You have quite an imagination for doom-and-gloom scenarios."

"That's my job. My imagination helps me always be prepared."

A FEW EVENINGS LATER, Laura opened her front door and her classmates streamed in, each with food to share. Oliver and Richard hauled a roaster with shredded chicken, Skip brought a vegetable tray, Brock and Allen brought chips and buns, Diane brought a chocolate cake on a big platter and Marshall brought two twelve-packs of pop.

"We're ready for an all-nighter," Diane declared.

"Is it going to take us all night to review for the test?" Laura asked.

"Honey, I haven't taken a test in over twenty years. Once I get past putting my name at the top, I'm afraid I'll freeze up."

"I'm not a great test taker, either," Marshall admitted. "I survived the police academy and I knew my stuff, but I sweated those tests."

The other members of the group didn't add anything, but they had shown up. Their presence said they were at least worried enough to attend the study session.

Laura helped set up the potluck banquet on the kitchen counter, and Nicole dug through the cabinets for plates and serving utensils. "Thanks for helping," Laura said. "This isn't even my house and I invited seven people over."

"It's for a good cause," Nicole said.

Laura waited while everyone got a plate of food and found a seat. Nicole had helped her set up an extra table, and they had dragged in chairs from other rooms.

"As far as test taking goes," Laura said, "you don't have anything to worry about. It's just a matter of being prepared." She smiled encouragingly at the group.

"There's a lot to remember," Brock said. "Types of hazards, department protocol, sheesh."

"That's why we're here," Laura said. "And the notes we've all taken are going to be very handy for us."

Laura refilled the chip bowls and drinks, then assigned each person a chapter from the manual and had them write down the five most important things, the five things they were afraid they would forget on the test and five questions to quiz the rest of the group with. She had already done chapters one and two, and she began to demonstrate for her classmates so they'd have an example.

Kevin walked in while Laura was modeling the study strategy, and he jumped in and answered one of her questions before she could tell him not to.

"You'll have to leave," she said. "This is an invite-only party no matter how much I like you."

He laughed and surveyed the food lined up on the table. "That cake looks good," he said.

"If you're very lucky, there will be a piece

left over for you when you bring my sister home later."

"We're going out of town, so we'll be late," Kevin said. "I could try a piece now."

Nicole hooked an arm through his. "I'll get him out of here so he stops bugging you," she said. "Good luck with your study group."

"Is Kevin a brother or cousin to Tony?" Brock asked after Kevin and Nicole left. "I know there are a bunch of those Ruggles on the department."

"Cousin," Laura said. "He's marrying my sister in a few weeks and the reception is at the station."

"So you'll sort of be related to the chief," Skip said. His tone wasn't malicious. He was eighteen and just figuring out the world as far as Laura could tell. Unlike many of her former students who'd been lackluster about school, Skip was refreshingly enthusiastic. He'd said he wanted to be a professional firefighter like his uncle on another department, but that was almost all she knew about him.

"Not really," Laura said.

Despite all the time the group had spent together, it was surprising they had shared very little about their personal lives. Gathering around a dining room table instead of sitting in industrial chairs at the fire station was nice, but she didn't want the talk to veer anywhere close to personal when it came to Tony. The last thing she would admit to her classmates was that his sweatshirt was folded on a chair in her bedroom because she was waiting for an opportunity to return it when no one would notice. It wouldn't look good for someone to see her returning a piece of the fire chief's clothing.

Laura handed out the study questions she'd written on index cards, hoping to turn the conversation back to the science and skills of firefighting. She liked her classmates and hoped to get to know them better, but they had to focus on the written test coming up in just days. Once past that obstacle, they would prepare for the practical test.

"Work on your chapters, get help from your neighbor if you want, and I'll be here to help, too," she said. One of the most valuable things she'd learned from her time in the classroom was that students were much better off having to help themselves instead of having a teacher who did everything.

Tony didn't have a degree in education, but

he had been a very good teacher. It helped that the class was small, interested and a captivated audience. Tony had broken up the content into manageable chunks, provided appropriate materials and kept his lectures interesting with relevant anecdotes and regular trips out to the bays where the trucks and equipment waited. He even wrote his agenda on the whiteboard in the training room at the start of each class.

Laura had listened to every story Tony told, and his narratives showed his humility and compassion for the people he served. He had to possess his fair share of bravery, yet he didn't brag. If only there were more men in the world like Tony Ruggles. Men who cared about but didn't control others. Men who would give you their sweatshirt and a ride home whenever you needed them. A man who reserved judgment and would try to help you out of an awkward situation, even if you didn't remember to say thank you.

Oh, no. Her interactions with Tony going back a year did a quick scroll through her mind as if she were flipping through a year's worth of photographs on her phone. *No, no, no.*

She swallowed, afraid her face might give

away her thoughts, and excused herself. In the kitchen, she ran a paper towel under the faucet and grabbed the tall kitchen trash can. She counted to twenty and regulated her thoughts with each beat.

"Cleanup run," she announced as she went back into the dining room. "Round one."

As she wiped crumbs from the table and scooped paper napkins into the trash can, Laura tried to clear away the troubling thought that she might be falling a little bit in love with Chief Tony Ruggles. Those feelings would torpedo her plans to join the fire service and reinvent her life, and she owed herself the chance to do those things. Caring about him would be a mistake.

CHAPTER THIRTEEN

"YOU'VE ALL PASSED the written test," Tony said with a grin at the beginning of class a week later.

"Really?" Brock asked, raising his gray-speckled eyebrows. "Everyone?"

Laura wasn't at all surprised, but she felt a glow of satisfaction nonetheless.

"In fact," Tony said, "when I scored them, I discovered your class average was the highest that I know of for new groups of volunteers."

As she looked around at her cohort, Laura saw smiles and high fives. Marshall reached over and patted her on the back. Even Allen looked pleased, his expression showing none of his usual guardedness. Laura had been surprised and happy when he'd shown up to her study session. Maybe the ice was cracking.

"Can we blow the sirens and pull the air

horns now?" Richard asked. "There should be some reward."

"Maybe we'll save that for the Fourth of July parade—which you're welcome to ride along in, by the way," Tony said. "But we *are* going to get in the trucks tonight and practice driving them. It isn't often our volunteers are asked to drive the pumper or the ladder truck. As you know, a lot of times we're already at a fire when we realize we need your help."

"I've always wanted to drive a fire truck," Diane said.

Tony laughed. "I remember you saying that on the first night. And guess what? You get to go first."

"Is it a stick shift?" Diane asked. "My sister had a Toyota with a standard transmission, and I learned to drive one back in college. I think I still remember."

"Believe it or not, a lot of fire trucks come with an automatic. All of ours do. We traded off the last one with a standard two years ago. You have plenty of other things to worry about on the way to a call, so it's nice that you don't have to shift gears while trying to stay safe, hurry and dodge tourists, too."

"This is going to be great," Marshall said. "Defensive driving with the police cars was one of my favorite parts of the police academy."

Gavin stuck his head in the door. "All set up, Chief."

"Thanks," Tony said. "Everybody ready? We've got cones set up on the apron behind the station where we're not likely to have an audience. We'll take you one at a time and go through a course forward and backward. It's not easy, but if you go slow and use your mirrors, we'll get you through it."

Laura had been looking forward to this part of the training, too. There was something about those trucks that fired on all her sensory cylinders. The sound, sight and smell were tangible signs that someone who could help had arrived. She liked the trucks in the same way that she liked shopping for school supplies for her classrooms. Stacking up books, folders and erasers with their distinctive textures and aromas made the process of education seem as if it were something she could touch.

Beyond the equipment, the fire service remained tangible whereas teaching did not.

Instead of wondering if her words and lessons would change students' lives at some distant point in the future, her actions as a member of the fire department would have an immediate effect. Flames could be extinguished. Lifesaving oxygen administered. A crash victim removed from a mangled car. Real results in real time.

"You have all taken part in three or four Sunday inspections, so you know the trucks, but driving them is different," Tony said as he stood outside next to the open driver's door of the first pumper. "It's a great responsibility—"

"But awesome," Gavin interjected.

Tony laughed. "He's not wrong."

Laura heard nervous laughter around her. She wondered if anyone else in the group had ever driven such a large, expensive or important piece of machinery. She'd driven the eight-passenger van to a few cross-country meets when there weren't enough participants to warrant a giant school bus. She'd had to pass a short test and show her proof of insurance, but that was nothing like this.

"See that line of cones?" Tony said, pointing to about a dozen orange traffic cones lined up in a curving pattern. "All you have to do is stay on the right side of the cones on the way down the line and then the left side on the way back."

"Easier said than done," Oliver said. "I had to do something like this with a forklift at the plant and get certified. I was more nervous than when I was sixteen, going for my driver's license."

"Which time?" his brother asked. "The first try or the third?"

"Hey," Oliver said. "That guy had it in for me. I swear I didn't hit that bird on purpose."

"Barring birds and nerves, you'll be fine," Tony said. "I'll ride shotgun with each of you, but I won't offer suggestions unless you ask. Remember, there was a first time for all of us, and now driving these big trucks is second nature."

Laura wasn't sure it would ever be as easy as squeezing her hatchback into a parking space at the grocery store, but she appreciated Tony's attempt to put everyone at ease. It was one of the many things she…liked… admired about him. She quickly put that thought out of her head because she had to focus on what she was doing, not on why she should not have feelings for the fire chief. If she wanted to reinvent her life, she had to remain in control of it.

Diane climbed into the driver's seat and Tony walked around the front of the truck and got in on the other side. Diane leaned out the window. "Do you have to watch? It'll make me nervous."

"We're not looking," Richard said. "We're just standing here talking about the weather."

Diane shook her head, then pulled on her seat belt.

"Gotta love her spirit," Allen said quietly behind Laura.

"In a minute we might be awestruck by her incredible driving skills," Laura said. She stepped back so she was shoulder to shoulder with Allen. "Have you ever driven anything like this?"

"My grandpa's farm truck. It was huge, but as long as it had farm license plates, you didn't need a special license to drive it. I used to help him haul stuff at harvest time."

"That was nice," Laura said.

Allen shrugged. "Got me out of a day of school. Sometimes a whole week."

"You didn't like school?" He reminded her

of Adam suddenly. Adam had not enjoyed school and had relied heavily on her help, but he'd dutifully gone to college freshman year because their parents had saved up money and expected it. Laura had thought the fire service would be a much better choice for him.

"My class's five-year reunion was last weekend," Allen said, "and I mowed my lawn and edged my sidewalk instead of going. I'm sure they could all manage to sit around and admire themselves without my help."

"That's the thing I hated about school as a student and a teacher. That front some people put up where they act like they know something you don't and are somehow more important. I know it's just insecurity, but it's hard to overlook. But guess what," Laura said. "None of those people from high school are here tonight. If they were, I think they'd be admiring you."

Allen laughed. "Wait until I make it down those lines without a cone massacre before you give me too much credit."

Diane missed all the cones on her forward drive down the line. On the reverse, she oversteered, going too wide and then too narrow. She only took out two cones, and Tony said it was one of the better first attempts he'd seen.

The men in the class each took a turn, and Brock was the first one to have a perfect run of no knocked-over cones. "I drove the dump truck for the city sometimes," he said. "It's a little smaller, but the same idea."

Laura was the last person to climb into the pumper. When she pictured racing to someone's rescue, she always imagined herself interacting with accident victims or going into a burning building and saving a child or at least a family pet. She did not think of herself weaving through summertime traffic in Cape Pursuit. Not being a local—not yet, anyway—she hardly knew her way around town. She could get to work, the art gallery and the gym, but there was no way she was going to pass a quiz over street names.

As she climbed into the driver's seat, she vowed to memorize a map of at least the main streets of Cape Pursuit. What if someone's life depended on her? The thought that she could get lost and let someone down took a slice out of her usual confidence. Or maybe it was being alone in the cab with Tony where he would scrutinize her every move and her fitness for driving the fire truck.

He might physically see her hands clenching the wheel, but at least he wouldn't be able to read her thoughts. Letting him have any idea that her feelings for him had taken a somewhat reckless path wouldn't inspire his confidence in her ability to handle an emergency. Admitting her attraction to him would be its own disaster and there was no way to train or prepare for such a thing.

Professional. Keeping it light and distant between them was her only saving grace. If she was going to join the department, it had to be on her terms and for the right reasons. It couldn't involve feelings between her and the fire chief.

As she put the truck in gear, avoiding looking at Tony who sat forward with one hand on the dashboard, she thought back to the early summer day on the beach when she had suddenly known what she had to do. If she channeled that focus and determination to make the difference in someone else's life, she could weave through cones forward and backward.

"You can do this," Tony said, and Laura took her eyes off the course to shoot him a quick glance. He wasn't trying to distract her. He was just Tony. A nice guy who encouraged other people so hard she almost wondered…who had his back and pep-talked him when he had a bad day? Did he have bad days? She wished she knew him well enough to ask.

"Do you think you should turn on the siren and blow the horn so this is a more realistic experience?" Laura asked as she carefully inched the truck forward and followed the curving line of cones. So far, so good.

"Realistic, but tough on our neighbors."

The buildings surrounding the fire station were mostly light commercial, but there was a street full of houses just one block over.

"You don't think they're used to sirens?" Laura asked. She came to a stop at the end of the line of cones and got ready to shift into reverse for the more challenging half of the course.

"I hope not. I don't want anyone to get so accustomed to sirens that they tune them out. That would be dangerous for everyone involved."

Getting immune to things is how a lot of people survive their days. Laura had tried numbness as a way to cope with her brother's death and the hollow expressions on her parents' faces. It only worked to a point. She'd gotten out of bed every day, gone to work or practice or the grocery store, paid her bills on time and made regular visits to her dentist. But she had been hollow, too.

Firefighting was already filling her up, but she had to be careful not to let her feelings for Tony muddle the genuine spark she felt from preparing to serve her community. The short romances of the previous year had seemed to fill an empty place, too, but that warmth hadn't lasted, and Laura knew it was no substitute for her own peace of mind and emotional health.

"You're doing fine," Tony said.

IT WASN'T HOT in the cab, but Tony felt a bead of sweat roll down his back. He could blame the stress of creeping through an obstacle course with beginner drivers in a half-million-dollar truck. Eight times. But their driving hadn't been frightening. They were all too intimidated by the size of the truck to go fast, and there were only a few squashed cones that would probably regain their original shape.

And he hadn't been sweating until the last driver.

"You helped everyone in your class make that test look easy," he said. "Kevin told me about the study session at your house."

"Don't all your groups get together to review before the test?" Laura asked, never taking her eyes off the side mirror as she backed around a cone. "It's the logical thing to do."

"Not that I know of," he said. "This group was lucky to have a teacher in it."

"Rats," Laura said. "I nudged a cone."

Tony glanced in the mirror on his side of the truck. "You didn't knock it over, so I'd say it doesn't count."

"You're just being nice."

"No, but I do feel bad for distracting you by talking to you." He'd sat in silence with the other drivers, only offering advice if he thought they were going off course. With Laura, he had a more personal relationship, even though he felt as if he were playing with fire whenever he was near her.

"It's okay if you talk to me. I'm good at handling distractions. As a teacher, I had to be."

Tony noticed her use of past tense for her teaching career. "It's a good skill for the fire service, too," he said.

Laura cleared the last cone without running it over and stopped. She kept a foot on the brake after she finished the course.

"I wonder if you're sure about leaving teaching," Tony said. "I mean, there are schools in this area. You could move here and continue being an educator."

Laura put the truck into park and leaned back in the seat. "I'm trying to decide what I'd do if you came to me and said you were giving up being a firefighter," she said.

Tony laughed. "Never going to happen."

"There you go," she said, gesturing with both hands. "That kind of incredible certainty that you're doing exactly what you're meant to do is something I want to find. Need to find. For myself."

"I'm sorry," he said. "It's none of my business."

He didn't get involved in the personal lives of the other volunteers, even though he knew some facts about them, such as where they worked or if they were married. Being with Laura made him want to know more about her, know her better. Even if those feelings were dangerous. Earlier in the summer, he'd been curious about her, but since then she had interested him in a different way. He wanted to help her, protect her.

That was a tough job when he was supposed to be preparing her to learn to protect other people, even at her own risk.

"Is this how you set the air brakes?" she asked, her hand on a knob near the steering wheel.

Tony realized he'd been staring at her instead of keeping his mind on his work. "It is," he said. "Good call, since you're the last driver. Let's get out and I'll demonstrate how to use the wheel chocks to make double sure this thing doesn't roll while on a fire scene."

Tony bailed out the door and breathed a little easier when he was no longer in a confined space with Laura. He heard one of the guys congratulating her on not knocking over any cones, and her response admitting to nudging one. Even though she and Diane were the first women to pursue being part of the Cape Pursuit Fire Department, neither one of them seemed to approach the job as if they had something to prove.

The jury was still out on the two younger guys, Skip and, especially, Allen, but Tony was glad about the overall attitude of the group. They weren't out for personal glory. They just wanted to help and be part of something positive.

"Here," he said, opening the side compartment of the truck right over the rear wheels. "This is where we keep the chocks. You always, always use them. I don't care if you're on the flattest street in the world. You never take a chance on a truck this size rolling on you. Can't trust parking brakes, can't trust anything except your own attention to detail and safety."

He pulled out the hard rubber blocks and tossed them on the ground behind the wheels. "Go ahead," he said, pointing to Oliver and Diane. "Kick them into place with your foot. Make sure they're not going to go anywhere."

He watched them secure the wheel chocks and then he motioned for the group to go around the other side of the truck where he had two different people repeat the action. "The ambulance is one exception to this rule. It's not as heavy, and you're not likely to stay on scene very long. Obviously, you'd have to use your judgment if you got in a messy situation or had to park on a hill. The ladder truck is different, too. In addition to chocking the wheels, you absolutely must put out the outriggers."

"Are we doing that tonight?" Marshall asked.

Tony shook his head. "That's a whole other class. One of these nights or Sunday mornings, we'll put up the ladder, but it's not for the faint of heart. Let's go ahead and pull these wheel chocks out now, different people than who put them in. Store them back where they go, and then I'm going to need a volunteer to pull the truck into the station."

Allen stepped forward, one hand raised. "I'll do it," he said.

Tony was pleased to see Allen participate, and he was very happy someone other than Laura had volunteered first. Tony would have to sit in the passenger seat with whoever was putting the truck away, and he wasn't sure he could handle the heat of being that close to Laura for the second time that evening.

As the chief of the department, the last thing he could do was have any talk of a personal relationship with a woman on the roster. He didn't know if there was an official regulation against it, because it had never come up before. Who would have imagined that a smart, beautiful, determined woman would breeze into Cape Pursuit for the summer and that she would find her way to his office, asking to join?

The fire service seemed to be something she wanted to be part of so badly that it was a need more than a want. If he showed too much interest in her, it would make her uncomfortable. He couldn't drive her away, so he had only one choice.

He had to keep her at an emotional distance no matter how much he wondered what she would feel like in his arms.

CHAPTER FOURTEEN

LAURA WAVED TO the people lined up on the sidewalks of downtown Cape Pursuit. Only a few of the volunteers had decided to ride along in the Independence Day parade because many of them had family plans for the holiday. The fire department had supplied two pumpers, a ladder truck, a rescue truck and one ambulance for the parade, and the rest of the long lineup included police cars, floats built by local groups and members of a local horse club. The fire equipment was staged at the beginning and the end of the parade so they could leave easily in the event of an emergency.

The parade was similar to the ones Laura had looked forward to every year back home. Laura's school always sent a contingent of teachers in matching T-shirts to march right behind the high school band. Her cross-country team usually rode on a float or in the back of a pickup truck, and Laura had split her time between representing the team and the teaching staff.

And now she was representing the Cape Pursuit Fire Department, a new turn in her life that filled her with both nervous and happy excitement.

Her sister had told her that the biggest parade of the year was the one in August for the annual homecoming festival, but the July Fourth one had drawn a decent crowd despite the summer heat. She considered the bucket of candy in her lap and decided to be a bit more conservative so she wouldn't run out before the end of the parade.

"Are you sure you won't let me drive?" Laura asked. "At this speed, how much trouble can I get into?"

Jane's husband, Charlie, laughed as he kept one hand on the wheel and waved out his window. "It's not about you getting in trouble, it's me. The chief would have my head if I let you drive before you're an official member. Next year, it's all yours. I'll be sitting in the shade having a cold one while you sweat it out and creep along in this parade."

Next year. Laura took a deep breath, inhaling the scent of the fire station that clung to the trucks. She noticed the smell of tires, trucks and an old watery smoke scent in her hair when her head hit the pillow after an evening at the station. The scent had come to mean empowerment and belonging. Would she still be there next year for the parade? Even though she knew what she was *not* going to do when the end of the summer came, did she know what she would do?

Charlie switched on the siren and gave three long blasts of the air horn. Little kids in the audience either clapped their hands over their ears or waved wildly at the truck. Some of them bent their arms and pulled down, the universal sign for honking an air horn.

"I have no idea why people love parades," Charlie added. "Big loud trucks driving slowly, high school bands that only know three songs and people shaking hands running for office." He made a sound of disgust.

"I love parades," Laura said. She flung a handful of candy toward a group of kids waiting with grocery store bags draped over their arms. "You need something sweet." She handed Charlie a wrapped chocolate. "You'll feel better."

"Thanks," he said. "I got fifteen minutes of sleep last night because our baby has decided to get teeth."

"You'll be glad when she uses those teeth to eat real food," Laura said. "She'll sleep through the night, then."

"Always a silver lining," Charlie said. "Although she's beautiful, even when she's fussing all night. Wouldn't trade her for anything."

Laura's sister had filled her in on the events of the previous summer when Jane had discovered she was having a baby with someone who had been her best friend for years. Their friendship had taken a wild turn for just one night, but that night had redirected the course of their lives. Judging from Jane's happiness and Charlie's obvious joy at being a father, Laura thought their lives had clearly changed in a wonderful way.

"Are you on duty all day?" she asked.

He nodded. "We run a pretty full shift on July Fourth because the good people of Cape Pursuit become total morons when it comes to booze and fireworks. A guy burned the back porch off his house last year, and one time we had a fool try to shoot fireworks from a moving car."

"Oh, my gosh," Laura said. "How did that turn out?"

"Wasn't pretty." Charlie smiled and waved at people on the parade route. "The guy had the launcher backward and shot the fireworks into his own car. The seat caught fire and he drove into a ditch."

"That's terrible," Laura said, smiling and waving despite the dangerous story.

"Could have been a whole lot worse," Charlie said. "I can't wait to see what happens tonight."

"Maybe you'll get lucky and everyone will be at the park watching the official fireworks shot off by professionals. I'm going with my sister and Jane and the baby."

"I'm jealous, but I wouldn't be much fun because I'd be sitting there wondering when I'm going to get called out," Charlie said.

As they neared the end of the parade route, Charlie turned off the flashing lights and dropped onto a secondary street. They drove to the station where Laura's bicycle was parked. The blue bike helmet she'd bought two weeks earlier dangled from the handlebars.

Laura slid out of the big truck and helped back Charlie in, even though she suspected he could easily have done it without her. The ladder truck, which she knew Tony had driven, was already back in its place, which meant Tony was probably there in the station. They hadn't been alone together since their conversation during the driving lesson, and Laura didn't know what to think about their relationship.

It was better not to think about it. Instead, she planned to put her energy into being an excellent volunteer.

"I wonder if there's anything I can do to help tonight," she said aloud to Charlie.

"Could be," he said. "I'm not exaggerating when I say we'll be busy. Last year, there was no one to run the radio here and we had to route all our traffic through central dispatch. It works, but it's a pain."

Tony came around the end of the truck. "You could come in tonight, if you want to," he said. "It might give you a taste of how crazy it can get sometimes."

Charlie grunted. "A bad taste."

"What time?" Laura asked.

"Whenever you'd like, but dusk is when people in Cape Pursuit seem to decide to cash in their life insurance policies," Tony said. "And make sure you drive your car tonight instead of riding your bike after dark. Too dangerous."

Had Tony noticed her bike outside? The fact that he cared made her feel special, but she reminded herself that he noticed everything and cared about everyone.

"I'll be here," she said.

Laura sought out her sister at the art gallery, where she and Jane were doing booming business after the parade. The baby slept in a playpen in the back room, and the shop was filled with people looking at Jane's paintings and Nicole's photography. Local points of interest including the shoreline, mermaid statue and lighthouse made excellent subjects for art, and tourists had given Sea Jane Paint a very good year so far. Laura was happy for her sister and her friend. They knew what they wanted to do, and they were enjoying hard-won success.

"I have to bow out of our plans for tonight," Laura said as she stepped behind the register and helped wrap a painting in heavy paper.

Nicole turned a questioning frown on her sister. "Is something wrong?"

"I volunteered to be on hand at the station."

Nicole opened her mouth and then closed it again as she taped the paper around the frame while Laura held it. Nicole ran the customer's credit card, completed the sale and smiled at the next person in line who was purchasing a set of hand-painted coasters.

"Sorry," Laura said quietly as she stood beside her sister. The customer paid cash and Laura slipped her purchase into a paper bag with a string handle.

"We were going to have fun," Nicole said. They were temporarily alone at the register. "I even had a plan for a picnic basket and some wine."

"I know, but Charlie was telling me it would be a busy night, and Tony said I could come help if I want. It's good experience."

"Experience for what?" Nicole asked. "For risking your life and exposing yourself to all kinds of dangerous, terrible things? You'd rather do that than spend your evening with me when I'm almost the only family you have?"

Laura wanted to reach out and hug her sister, but a woman came up to the register asking about a custom glass piece in the front window.

Nicole went to help the customer, and Laura stayed behind the register. An ache in her chest took the brightness out of the sunny day. Aside from her parents, Nicole was her only family. But the firefighters had begun to feel like her family, too, and she didn't want to leave them shorthanded. Now that she'd committed to helping at the station, she couldn't go back on her word.

Although she *had* broken plans with her sister who already considered Laura's desire to be a volunteer firefighter a betrayal. She wished there was a way she could be a good sister and also follow her heart.

The store stayed busy until Jane locked the door at five o'clock. "Kevin and Charlie are working at the station," Nicole told Jane, "and now Laura has decided to go there, too, so it's just us for the fireworks."

Jane flashed a tentative smile at Laura,

who stood nervously jingling the key to her bike lock. "More food for us, then," Jane said. "You'll miss out on the party at the park, but maybe you'll get lucky and get to ruin someone's fun by turning a hose on their homemade fireworks."

"Tony and Charlie didn't make it sound like fun," Laura said. She smiled at her sister who still looked angry.

"Just be careful," Nicole said.

Laura rode her bike back to the house alone. She changed into a pair of jeans but left on the navy blue fire department T-shirt Tony had given her and the other volunteers who were riding in the parade. It was just like the ones the other firefighters had, with a symbol and insignia of the department on the front chest and the large letters CPFD on the back.

She considered grabbing the sweatshirt she'd borrowed from Tony the night of the 5K, but it wasn't the right time to return it with a station full of people. It hadn't seemed like the right time the last four training sessions, either. Tony had either forgotten about it, didn't care because he had five of them or he might think she was keeping it for a reason.

When she arrived at the station, she noticed that one of the ambulances was already out. All the station doors were open, and the missing vehicle left an empty spot.

"You drove," Tony said. He smiled at her, and Laura wondered if he was pleased she had done as he'd asked or if he was just glad to see her. Or in a holiday mood. "Good. Let me show you how to run the radio in case this year is anything like the last ten. I hate the Fourth of July."

So, not a holiday mood, Laura decided as she followed Tony into a small office filled with maps and equipment. She had only been in there one other time during a Sunday morning truck inspection, but she remembered thinking it was like command central.

"Can you control the weather from in here?" she asked.

"If I could, I'd make it rain tonight so people would go home, have a nice dinner and watch the fireworks from Washington, DC, on television."

"That sounds dull."

"But safe," he said. He pointed to the detailed street map of Cape Pursuit under a clear plastic desktop. "You might want to study this sometime. It has all the water mains and hydrants marked. Not a bad idea to get an understanding of their pattern so you can plan ahead on the way to a call."

"In addition to running the siren and not running over tourists and stray animals."

"You're never alone," Tony said, his face serious despite Laura's attempt to lighten the mood. "You always have a partner, always have backup, always make sure someone knows where you are." Laura nodded. That camaraderie was one of the major things missing from her life back home. Her parents had their own relationship, both with each other and with their grief. Her colleagues at school had kids and dogs. But Laura had often felt she was the lone swimmer in a giant ocean.

She ran her fingers over the clear plastic and tried to establish a pattern of which sides of the road hydrants were on and which neighborhoods flowed into which. Her sister had questioned her habit of going out driving after dinner several nights a week, but she explained that she was familiarizing herself with the street names and the complex maze of one-way streets in parts of the oceanfront town.

"I heard you backed out of your plans with Nicole and Jane tonight," Tony said.

Laura glanced up quickly, wondering how Tony knew.

"Charlie told me," he said. "You didn't have to do that."

"But you need help here," she said.

"You can't drop everything and abandon your family just because we might have a crazy night."

"That's what you do," she said.

Tony bit his lower lip and Laura thought she'd made an excellent point he couldn't argue with.

"My family is here," he said. "The name Ruggles is all over the roster board out there."

Maybe he could argue with her point.

"Well," she said. "Even if I'm the only Wheeler on the board, I can at least do my part tonight. Maybe I'll be helpful or I'll learn something. Fireworks are fireworks, and if things end up being quiet around here, I'll watch them on the television in the break room."

Tony blew out a breath and looked at Laura as if he was trying to figure her out. Laura didn't think she was complicated. In fact, she'd been trying to be an open book all summer, telling people exactly what she wanted and explaining why as best she could.

"Our radio is our lifeline," Tony said, pointing to a series of switches and colored lights. "Of course there's a 911 dispatcher who sends us out, and we communicate with dispatch when we leave the station and get on scene so there's a record. We can ask them to call mutual aid for us, too."

"It's good to know they're always listening," Laura said.

"Yes. But sometimes we need to call back to the station for more manpower or equipment, and it's nice to have someone here listening."

She nodded and sat at the desk where a computer display replayed the fire department logo in an endless bouncing screen saver.

"You can look up any address with that system. We know pretty much where everything is in this town, but there are always surprises. That program gives you details you didn't even know you needed."

Laura jiggled the mouse and typed in the address of the home she shared with Nicole. The readout stunned her in its detail. "Three bedrooms, two baths, a kitchen and a long narrow hallway. It also describes our back porch, the two-car garage and the gas meter outside the basement window."

"Like I said, details. Your house is pretty standard, but this information comes in handy when there are hazards like stored gasoline or a hidden cistern on the property. Even a mean dog. We don't like surprises."

"This seems personal," Laura said, looking at the picture of the outside of her house and the description of her gas furnace, central air and narrow attic with no entrance.

"It's business," Tony said, leaning over her.

With Tony so close, Laura could see the faint blond stubble on his chin and the fine lines around his eyes from the Cape Pursuit sunshine. He smelled like aftershave and the fire station, just as the sweatshirt that was still on a chair in her bedroom did. She was trying very hard to maintain a line in her heart between her personal feelings for Tony and her passion for becoming a valued member of the fire department.

It wasn't about her. It was about what she could do for others and finding her place in a world that had been turned upside down and sideways by Adam's death. No matter how appealing Tony was, caring for him would be a stumbling block she didn't need.

"Tell me how to operate this," she said.

Tony rolled a chair over and sat next to her. He reviewed the call letters and customary radio lingo, showed her where the numbers of all the trucks were written down and ran through the procedure for calling in or extending mutual aid with other departments. As usual, his explanation was detailed and supplemented with anecdotes from fire calls in the past. He was an excellent teacher— all the best teachers loved their subjects passionately.

She had once loved history, but seeing the blank interest from high school sophomores had chipped away at her passion for it. Gradually, she'd realized it wasn't history she loved—it was the idea of making a difference in someone else's life.

That realization meant she had to walk away from high school and do the one thing that both challenged her painfully and filled her heart.

A sharp tone emanated from the radio and a dispatcher's voice came on. Laura jumped in her seat and pulled her hands back from the radio.

Tony laughed. "You didn't do anything."

They both listened carefully to the dispatcher's description of the emergency and the location. Tony picked up the mic and confirmed the message with the dispatcher. Laura's heart was pounding, and Tony was so close she imagined he must be able to hear it.

"Heart attack. And one ambulance is already out," Tony said. "Looks like it's going to be one of those nights."

Laura heard movement and doors slamming out in the bay. Tony hopped up and went out, Laura on his heels.

"Got your fire gear?" Tony asked Charlie and Travis who were in the cab of the ambulance.

They both nodded and Tony gave them the thumbs-up sign.

"Will they need fire gear on this call?" Laura asked.

"No, but they may not make it back here before the next one comes in. Always better to be prepared."

"So I may be driving the fire truck and meeting them somewhere?" Laura asked, smiling at Tony.

"Not yet," he said. He crossed the station and went into the bunk room on the other side. Something about the way he said *not yet* instead of *no* made Laura feel as if she'd already passed a test. She went back into the radio room, determined to investigate the computer program further and memorize the call numbers of all the trucks. She hoped it would become second nature to her the longer she stuck around.

However long that was going to be.

Laura listened to the radio traffic from the newest ambulance call and recognized Charlie's voice reporting to dispatch that the ambulance was en route. At the same moment, she heard the backup alarm on the other ambulance as it reversed into the station. With five overhead doors on the front and rear of the station, ten pieces of emergency equipment could face outward at all times and be ready for a quick exit. She could picture exactly where that ambulance was backing in and filling one of the slots.

She wanted to go out and ask what the call had been. Listening to stories about emergencies and asking questions about what the responders had done was a great way to learn. Tony had recommended it to everyone in her class. Listen and ask questions. Excellent advice.

Laura was about to leave the radio room when she heard Charlie say something she didn't understand. Code fifteen. What was a code fifteen? Had she heard that signal before? She listened more closely as Charlie confirmed the code for the dispatcher and gave the address. Whatever a code fifteen was, Charlie had seen and reported it.

"Dumpster fire," Tony yelled, his voice echoing in the station. "Outside a vacation rental complex, close to a structure. Charlie called it in."

Laura heard truck doors slamming and men talking, and then Tony's voice. "Laura, tell the dispatcher message received."

She had abandoned the radio to stand in

the doorway and watch three firefighters get in the pumper, but she ran back in and did as Tony asked. She hoped her nervous excitement wouldn't show in her voice. She heard the pumper roar out of the station, its siren switching on a moment later, another truck right behind it.

Silence in the station. How many men had been on duty when she arrived? Two were out but had returned and gone again with Tony on the pumper. Charlie and Travis were out. Was it just her? Laura picked up a portable radio and did a quick sweep of the station.

As she peeked in the empty bunk room, she knew how many men had gone. All of them.

For thirty long minutes, Laura paced and listened as Tony's voice narrated his arrival on scene, announced the fire was under control and there was no structural damage other than to the dumpster. *That was fast.* Tony sounded as if putting out a fire was something he did every day, like brushing his teeth or setting his alarm clock. Laura was relieved and reassured to hear his voice.

The bay doors were wide open to the sunset. She kept the radio in hand as she wandered the empty station and breathed a sigh of relief when she heard Charlie tell dispatch his ambulance was returning to the station because the patient had refused transport. Laura wasn't afraid of being alone, and she wasn't afraid to face an emergency, but she knew there was very little she could do except call in another department if something happened.

"I phoned in a pizza order on our way back," Charlie said as soon as he and Travis got out of the ambulance. "I just hope we have time to eat it."

"I hope you ordered a lot," Laura said. "I've burned a thousand calories just listening to the radio."

"We always order a lot," Travis said.

An hour later, the rest of the crew returned. As they ate lukewarm pizza, Laura got Kevin to tell her all about the dumpster fire. His description made it sound routine, no big deal. They pulled a hose off the pumper, knocked out the fire, wrote a report in conjunction with the police who had been called to that location after earlier reports of fireworks in the parking lot, and left.

"Hardly got our hands dirty," Kevin said. "But I doubt our luck will hold."

As he spoke, they all heard fireworks crackling in the night sky. Loud booms and hissing streamers infiltrated the station.

"The city show has begun," Charlie said.

"It sounds spectacular," Laura said. "The shows back home often had big gaps between each shell. This one goes on and on."

Tony sat down across from Laura and cracked open a can of soda. "It sure does. And then people get in fender benders leaving the park or, worse, hurry home and set off their own firecrackers."

"Maybe this will be the year absolutely nothing bad happens and you'll sleep like babies," Laura said.

"Babies don't actually sleep," Charlie said. "I know this from experience."

Signal tones for a call echoed through the station and Tony held up his radio so they could all hear the report from dispatch about a fireworks injury and a fire at a home on the other side of Cape Pursuit. Tony acknowledged the call in motion as he and the other firefighters ran out the door.

Laura watched the ambulance, the pumper

and the rescue truck roll out of the station, flashing lights and sirens activated. Over the radio, she heard Tony call out the volunteers and ask them to stand by at the station. She went into the radio room, wishing there was more she could do. Laura watched the second hand tick around the face of the clock, hoping the fire trucks and ambulance would get there soon.

Tony's voice informed dispatch they were on scene with flames showing and at least one critical injury. Glued to the radio, Laura waited for more information. She heard volunteers and off-duty firefighters come in, talking in the bay. Tyler Ruggles, Kevin's brother, was one of them. Laura looked out and saw him and Gavin taking off in the secondary pumper with two men in the back.

Over ten minutes went by before Laura heard Kevin's voice on the radio informing dispatch the ambulance was leaving the scene en route to the hospital. He sounded calm, sober. Whatever had happened to the person, it had to be terrible if Tony had described the injuries as critical.

If I were there right now, what would I be doing?

Laura absorbed everything she heard on the radio and meshed it with the hours of classroom and practical instruction she'd experienced in the previous weeks. Would she have what it takes in an actual emergency? If she had to save a life, would she know what to do?

Another half hour went by, and she heard Kevin tell dispatch the ambulance would be returning to the scene. Did that mean there were other injuries, or were the firefighters at risk? Was Tony okay? She hadn't heard his voice on the radio for what seemed like a long time.

Finally, nearing midnight, Tony radioed dispatch and announced they were leaving the scene. His tone was calm, but it didn't have the notes of reassurance she had come to expect. It sounded more like resignation... as if he'd done the best he could and failed.

She waited, anxiously. Several volunteers who had manned the station in case of another call had stuck around, too. What was the protocol for a situation like this? Could she ask Tony or one of the other guys for details? He'd encouraged all the new volunteers to ask questions and listen, but did that apply right on the heels of an ugly fire call?

"What kind of a mess did you have out there?" one of the volunteers asked as soon as Kevin stepped down from the truck. Laura still had the portable radio in her hand, but she had given up her seat in the radio room. She was relieved that someone else had jumped in and asked the question so she could listen in.

"Crappy one. Half the house is burned out, and the guy who owns it blew off his hand with fireworks. His timing must have been way the heck off and he had only a stub left. Bleeding bad," Kevin said. He shook his head, looking miserable but stoic.

The volunteer who had asked covered his mouth and ran for the bathroom. Kevin half smiled. "Troy doesn't like blood and can't handle the medical stuff, but he's a great fire-fighter so we're happy to have him around."

Laura couldn't help imagining what a long road the victim would have ahead of him. "Do you think the hospital can…reattach it?"

Kevin shook his head. "Sometimes they can, but in this case, we couldn't find enough… parts."

"Got hose to clean," Tony said. "You okay, Laura?"

"Sure, yes."

Kevin walked away and Tony looked seriously at Laura, scrutinizing her. "It's hard at first, facing the terrible things that happen to other people or that they do to themselves."

She nodded. She'd faced some terrible things...that morning the men had stood on her parents' doorstep with the worst news.

"But you deal with it by knowing you're doing the best you can to make things better," Tony said. "Being able to do something takes the bite out of even the worst situation."

Laura smiled for the first time in hours and felt a weight lift from her shoulders. "That's exactly why I'm here," she said.

Tony drew his eyebrows together and a question crossed his face, but then he looked as if he'd realized something. "Now I get it."

When Laura arrived home that night, her sister was already in bed. Laura knew she would have to mend fences with Nicole the next day for choosing the fire department over her, but if she could put into words the

way she felt, maybe Nicole would understand.

Maybe she would use Tony's words, because they were exactly right.

CHAPTER FIFTEEN

TONY HESITATED. HE'D been about to call Laura's personal cell phone. If she had been a male volunteer for the department, he wouldn't have batted an eye. If he had as much personal interest in her as he had any of his other firefighters, it would have been easier. But Laura did interest him. She tested him. She made him question his own motives.

These motives were pure. This phone call was not because he waited for Laura to walk into the room every night of training or sensed her presence wherever she was in the fire station. Or thought about her at night as he was trying to go to sleep. This phone call was good for Laura and the department in general.

He tapped in the number she'd written on her volunteer application. It was midmorning, the day after Independence Day. Would she be at work? He expected and almost hoped his call would go straight to voice mail. He tried to summon the courage that sustained him in the face of fires, accidents and disasters.

Laura's voice came on the line, a question in her "Hello?"

"It's Tony," he said, even though he assumed she had caller ID and wouldn't have answered the phone for just anyone. He hoped she wouldn't.

"You're calling from the fire station," she said. "Is everything okay?"

"Everything's fine. I'm calling to ask a favor."

He wouldn't ask for himself, but he was willing to stick his neck out for the department. He hoped Laura would say yes, but he didn't want to make her feel obligated.

"Okay," Laura said. "What can I do to help you? You don't have to write a speech or a toast or something like that for my sister's wedding, do you?"

He laughed. "Maybe a toast, but Kevin's brother has speech duty. And the wedding is two weeks away."

"Plenty of time," Laura said.

Tony sat on the bench in front of the fire station. The friendly back and forth was throwing him off balance, so he focused on the concrete Dalmatian wearing a red fire helmet. The statue had been a gift years ago to the station and it sat right outside the front door.

"Are you available for lunch tomorrow?" he asked abruptly, suddenly wanting to get the question asked and answered before he got any more nervous.

There was a long pause before she answered, and Tony realized he'd steered the conversation in a backward, stupid way. What if she thought he was asking her for a lunch date?

"Actually, no," Laura said. "I promised Nicole we'd have lunch tomorrow, and I can't stand her up again after last night. She's still mad about me joining the fire service and last night didn't help."

"Breakfast?" Tony asked.

"I think you should tell me what's on your mind," Laura said, her tone amused but curious. "And then I'll decide which meals I could commit to."

Tony smiled. Laura was savvy enough

not to let herself get into a situation without knowing what was going on. That made him feel better about her general safety and well-being, even though he didn't think of himself as dangerous. He swallowed. Were his feelings for Laura potentially messy enough to get in the way of her fire service? He didn't want to be the step over which she stumbled. She deserved this chance.

"An interview," he said. "With the local paper. A reporter saw you and Diane in the parade yesterday and started asking questions. When he found out that we have two female volunteers for the first time ever, he called the station and asked to do a story on you."

"On me and Diane."

"If she'll agree," Tony said.

"Have you asked her?"

"No. I started with you because I know you…"

Silence on the other end of the line did not help Tony after he left his words hanging. He meant to say he knew her better, but how would Laura interpret that?

"Are you asking me to call Diane and talk her into it?" Laura said.

"I'm asking for your opinion and your help. Do you want to do this interview? Would it make you uncomfortable to be singled out because of your…because you're a…"

"Woman," Laura said. "And no, it doesn't bother me. It just came out of the blue. I don't know what Diane will say, but if you want me to, I'll call her. I'm afraid she'll balk at the special attention, but she might view it as good for the department. I'll ask."

"Thank you," Tony said.

"You have to be there, too, of course," Laura said.

"At the interview?"

"Yes. And the interview has to be at the fire station, not just some restaurant somewhere."

Tony smiled, even though he knew Laura couldn't see it. She had a strong sense of how things should be and wasn't afraid to speak her mind.

"I can tell the reporter he has to bring lunch if he wants to talk to my hard-working volunteers," Tony said. "And take pictures."

"There will be pictures?"

"That's what he asked for."

He heard Laura sigh. "On second thought,

tell the reporter he doesn't have to bring lunch, but he does have to come to Tuesday night training and do a story on all the volunteers. Not just me and Diane."

Tony hesitated. It really was a milestone for the department to include women for the first time in its hundred-year history. But Laura had a point.

"He may not like it," Tony said. "But I'll tell him that's the deal."

"Good. Will you text me what he decides to do?"

"Sure."

After disconnecting, Tony called and gave the reporter his choices. All the volunteers or none of them. When the reporter quickly agreed, Tony knew Laura had been wise to suggest it. He pulled his personal cell phone from his pocket and texted Laura, who texted him back a smiley face. And he realized they'd just crossed a line into...friendship?

He didn't know what to call it, and he certainly didn't know what to do about it.

A FEW NIGHTS LATER, the reporter, Will York, showed up with a camera and a notebook just before class started.

"You picked a good time," Tony said. "The classroom part is over, and we're getting our hands dirty tonight." He pointed to a wrecked car he'd had hauled in from the junkyard. The car had clearly been involved in an accident and remnants of an airbag spilled over the steering wheel. The frame appeared to be sprung and the car crouched on the concrete with only one thing left to give.

"Our new recruits will learn how to use extrication tools to get someone out of a damaged car," Tony explained. "It'll be loud and messy, and you'll want to have your camera ready."

Tony had already moved both ambulances to the front side of the station so the concrete apron at the rear could serve as a training ground. He'd also asked a few of his longstanding volunteers to come help. It would be good for the newspaper story to also show a previous class of volunteers, and good experience for everyone involved.

As the eight new volunteers arrived and suited up, Tony talked with each of them and gave them a friendly warning about the reporter. He had considered calling to tell each of them in advance, but learning to deal with curious reporters was a reality of the fire service. Tony told each person they didn't have to give any statements unless they wanted to. Most of them shrugged good-naturedly, but Allen looked more grim and serious than usual. Laura already knew about the proposed article, and he guessed she'd called Diane, who didn't seem surprised by the news.

"It's hot, but you'll need full gear," Tony said. He put on his own turnout pants, coat and helmet, and waited while everyone suited up. He noticed the photographer taking pictures of Laura while she put on the protective clothing. Only Laura. Will York snapped dozens of pictures as she pulled up her turnout pants and slid her arms into her coat. He continued taking pictures as she snapped the coat shut and put on her helmet. Tony wanted to yank the camera out of York's hand and tell him Laura wasn't a museum attraction. She had the potential to be one of his best firefighters because she was determined and she paid attention. Was York taking those pictures because Laura was young and attractive?

Tony kept his irritation under control and

hauled equipment off the rescue truck. Hydraulic jaws and cutters, airbags and saws. Laura and Richard helped carry the equipment over to the already-damaged car, and Tony noticed the reporter taking more pictures of Laura. He wanted to step in front of her and protect her from the exposure; he considered sending her inside on an errand of some kind just to remove her from the situation. But then he reminded himself he couldn't protect her from everything, and she wouldn't want him to.

"If a victim's entrapped," Tony said to the assembled volunteers, "your job is to get them out quickly and safely. Any time you can shave off between the accident and getting the victim to a hospital may help save a life, but there are serious hazards with car accidents to both the victim and the first responders. You have to secure the scene. Is the car still running? Is it in danger of rolling or flipping? Any fire or leaking flammable fluids? You have to think about potential sparks from the equipment you'll be using."

Tony went over assessing the scene for hidden or obvious dangers in detail, then demonstrated how to hook up and run the hydraulic jaws. The volunteers gathered around as he showed them how to use the jaws to pop open one of the doors. Tony noticed the photographer hung back in the crowd and didn't take any pictures of him demonstrating the jaws. The article wasn't about the chief, and he'd been in the paper plenty of times. He expected the camera to come out as soon as he invited class members to work together to pop open the other three doors.

The hydraulic jaws were heavy, and it was hot work in full turnout gear. Tony stepped back and watched the volunteers team up. Sweat rolled down Brock's face as he and Allen forced a door open. Tony noticed Marshall helping Diane by lifting some of the weight of the tool as they worked together. Richard and Oliver started in on the third and last available door, but stopped and gestured for Laura and Skip to step up and take a shot at it.

When Laura's team approached the car, Tony watched her every move. She used her strength wisely and efficiently, and determination furrowed her brow. Her cheeks were pink with exertion, but her expression of triumph as she and Skip popped open their door was going to make an amazing picture for the newspaper. The photographer stood on the other side of the car and captured the entire thing.

Tony didn't know whether he wanted to grab the camera or let the reporter share Laura's beauty and will with everyone in the Cape Pursuit region. He wanted to keep her all to himself, he realized with a heart-stopping suddenness, but she wasn't his. And she never could be.

He cleared his throat and gathered everyone for the demonstration of the next piece of equipment, a hydraulic cutting tool. One of his older volunteers demonstrated how to cut the doorposts so that the roof could be folded back as Tony explained the procedure. The class of new volunteers took turns cutting doorposts, each of them making an individual attempt and cutting the posts in several places. Again, Tony noticed the photographer focusing on Laura.

Soon after, Laura came to stand next to Tony while others took their turns. Tony glanced at her, his voice low, and said, "Is that photographer bothering you?"

Laura turned her back on the rest of the people and the photographer so only Tony could see her face. "It's making me uncomfortable because he seems to be taking pictures of mostly me," she whispered.

"I noticed. Come into the station and help me grab waters for everyone," he said.

As they went inside, Laura said, "I thought you told him the story had to be about all the volunteers, not just the female ones."

"I did."

"That's not what he's doing."

"Believe me, I saw what he was doing." Tony couldn't keep the annoyance out of his voice, and he wondered what Laura would think had caused it. He didn't like to see anyone made uneasy, especially someone he cared about.

Laura pulled bottles of water from the fridge and handed six of them to Tony. "I almost don't want to go back out there," she said.

Tony put his bottles on the table. He wanted to pull Laura into his arms and hug her, but that would make a bad situation so much worse.

"It's not fair," Laura said.

"No, but you deserve to be out there doing your job. Truth be told, you're one of the best volunteers we've had in a long time. You're smart, you pay attention, and you're brave and dedicated."

She shook her head. "When you say things like that, it makes me feel…"

"What?" he asked gently. He wished he could see inside her thoughts.

"Afraid," she admitted, looking into his eyes. "Afraid of failing, of not knowing what to do and letting someone down at the worst time. Afraid everyone will find out I'm not as brave as I act."

Tony felt his heart pounding. How many times had he had the same thoughts?

"Now I know you're perfect for this," he said. "You just described everyone on this department, but you were actually brave enough to put it into words."

He wanted to tell her she was special to him and that he'd begun to care for her in a way that had nothing to do with the fire service, but now would be the wrong time. Heck, there would never be a right time.

"We're going to go back out there, and I'll tell that guy I want him to take lots of pictures of Marshall so the guys at the police station will give him crap about it."

Laura smiled, warming Tony's heart. She grabbed four bottles of water. "Let's go," she said.

CHAPTER SIXTEEN

"YOU CAN DO THIS," Tony said as he put heavy tape over Laura's mask. With each strip of tape, part of the world disappeared, and darkness made her feel more and more alone inside her fire gear. Was this what it felt like when Adam had finally given up running from the forest fire and pulled a fireproof blanket over himself? What were his final thoughts when he realized that, eventually, fire will always win?

Her breath quickened as Tony applied the last piece of tape, completely blotting out her view. Her battle was entirely hers to fight. She counted to slow her breathing. Two seconds in, three seconds out. The tube hanging from her mask wasn't hooked to the heavy air pack on her back yet, but when she faced her obstacle in a minute, it would be. If she hyperventilated, the air pack wouldn't last long enough for her to do what she had to do.

On the way to the state fire academy that morning, Tony had given her, Diane and Skip a ride, while the others carpooled with Kevin and Tyler. Tony had shared some tips about surviving the maze. It was a notorious proving ground for firefighters, and many people didn't conquer it on the first try.

She'd volunteered to go first for the maze while her classmates completed the other drills and exercises that constituted a final test for joining the fire service. They didn't have to get a 100 percent on any of the activities, but they were each aiming for a combined score of seventy points earned through the maze, a hose carry, a ladder test, hands-on CPR and a pump-operating test.

As Tony helped her suit up for the maze, Laura regretted choosing to tackle the hardest thing first. What if she failed and it killed her confidence for the entire day?

"Laura?" Tony asked. His voice was muffled. He patted her shoulders but she barely felt it through her heavy coat and the panic she was trying to force away with slow counting. "You can do this," he repeated, his voice sounding as if it was coming through water. "Nod if you're okay."

Laura bobbed her head up and down, feeling the weight of her fire helmet. She heard someone say *I believe in you*, and she didn't know if it was Tony or a voice in her own head. She felt Tony turn her by the shoulders and nudge her toward the entrance of the maze. No one in her volunteer class had seen inside the two-story maze, but they had all heard stories about it from other firefighters.

Staircases that were missing steps. Floors with holes large enough to fall through. Blocked doorways. Heavy obstacles. The two-hundred-pound dummy representing a victim waiting for rescue. Worst of all, complete darkness and senses muffled by heavy gear.

Someone hooked the hose from her mask to her air tank and she felt the subtle change as she drew life-saving air from the tank. Two loud taps on her tank told her it was time to go. She clutched a firehose in her left hand, dropped to her knees and put her right hand on the door frame. Right-hand search pattern, just as she had read about and practiced at the Cape Pursuit fire station. The lights had been on and the territory was familiar during the practice. This was entirely different, but she had to give it everything she had. If she could move quickly enough and not be overwhelmed by time, doubt, panic, fatigue or dangerous obstacles, she would eventually find the waiting dummy.

Then, she thought grimly, all she had to do was haul the dummy back out of the simulated house fire. They had practiced moving and carrying people in her training. In an awkward night of physical training, each of the volunteers had practiced picking up one of the others in a classic "fireman's carry." They all knew there was the possibility that they would have to use that knowledge someday and under the worst potential circumstances. The dummy waiting in the maze would outweigh her by sixty pounds, but Laura had training and determination on her side.

"Go, go, go." She didn't know who was yelling, but she was already moving as fast as she thought she could. *Maybe she could go faster.* It was hard. The heavy coat, boots, pants, gloves. The helmet like a cement block on her head. The air pack straining at her shoulders. And always, the breathing she had to control despite the exertion. If she breathed too fast and used up too much air, she would have to give up. Would fail. *Control.* It was something she had been groping for every day of the past two years.

Right hand on the wall, she searched the first room, sweeping out as far as she could with her left hand without losing her anchor hold on the wall. If she lost her bearings, how would she find them in the dark? There was nothing in the room except what felt like a couch. No dummy lying on the couch or curled beneath it. She went through a doorway and found herself in what she thought was a closet and then realized was a long hallway. She began to crawl. Her left knee dipped and she felt as if she were falling for a moment until she quickly lurched to her right to avoid the hole in the floor. She steadied her breathing, not willing to let the near-disaster derail her.

Searing heat met her at the end of the hallway and she had to turn. Tony had warned them there would be an industrial space heater simulating fire somewhere in the maze and they would have to make a difficult decision. She thought of Tony, waiting outside the maze, probably watching the clock. What was he thinking? Did he believe she could do it?

Which way? Reaching ahead of her, she counted, *One one thousand, two one thousand, three one thousand.* Had her brother's last moments been like this? Heat, darkness, panic that threatened to steal all your training and rob you of the power to think your way out?

No amount of thinking would have saved Adam. She knew that from the grim report delivered to her parents. No way out, there was nothing different he could have done. That two other men in his group had survived was a miracle, plain and simple.

Laura sat back, her boots digging into the backs of her thighs. Without thinking, her gloved hands batted uselessly against her mask. There was nothing she could do about the tears that fell as she thought of her little brother. She felt the moisture pooling at the bottom of her mask, and it didn't matter if the tears blinded her. There was nothing she could see with her mask covered in dark tape.

For a moment she considered ripping the

AMIE DENMAN

mask away. What was she doing? Why the hell did she think she could face the thing that had killed her brother and nearly destroyed her family? *One one thousand, two one thousand, three one thousand.*

Someone tapped on her air tank. Was that yelling?

Laura lurched forward. She was wasting time. If she didn't keep going and find the victim, he would die. *He would die.* Only she could find him. What if it was someone's father? Brother. Sister. Child.

She closed her eyes, useless as they were, put a hand on the wall, and started half crawling, half stumbling forward. She would find what she was looking for. She saw Adam's blond hair shining in the sunlight of a summer afternoon. Saw his smile. Heard his laughter mixed with the loud music he used to play in his bedroom right down the hallway from hers.

She forced herself down that hall, found a doorway, rushed through it and came across an obstacle. Hands flailing in front of her, she realized with a burst of joy that it was what she was looking for. The victim. The person she had to save. She fumbled to get the rescue strap from her pocket, looped it blindly around the dummy she found on the floor, and started moving backward toward the entrance.

Could she find where she had come in? She reviewed her pattern. How many rights had she taken? How many rooms? How far? As she passed by the heat source set up to simulate fire, she remembered. The maze laid itself out in her mind. She thought of Adam, imagined herself saving him despite the heavy weight, the burden. She left her fire hose behind, needing both hands to move the two-hundred-pound dummy.

She stumbled through a doorway and groped for a wall. *Oh, no.* There was no wall. Was she lost in the center of the maze with nothing to help her find a direction? She couldn't be. She couldn't let the victim die.

"Laura," a voice yelled next to her ear, but she couldn't process the sound. Who was yelling? Why was there someone else with her in the maze? "Laura, you did it!"

She was on her knees, unwilling to let go of the heavy weight she'd carried out of the maze. Bright light blinded her as someone ripped away a piece of tape from her mask. Was it really over?

Tony's smiling face appeared in front of her as another strip of tape was pulled away. Someone helped her to her feet and removed her helmet. She groped at the straps that held her face mask in place and pulled it off, tearing a few strands of hair with it.

"Are you okay?" Tony asked. He was the only person standing close enough to her to see the tearstains on her face and fresh tears in her eyes. Different tears. The first ones had been frustration, fear, loss and pain.

And then something had happened. She had found what she'd been looking for. Laura hadn't even realized she was crying tears of joy and triumph as she dragged that two-hundred-pound dummy through the maze to freedom. Survival.

She took a huge gulp of air. It was like breathing for the first time in a long time, like that first wonderful gasp when a swimmer comes up from the depths and breaks the surface.

"I'm okay," she said. She scrubbed the tears away. "Better than okay. I did it."

"You did it," he said. He put both hands on her shoulders and Laura thought he was going to put his arms around her, pull her into a tight hug. She took a huge step backward. If he hugged her at that moment after the emotional catharsis and physical exertion she'd just been through, she knew she would come apart.

In going through the maze, she had proven that she was capable of keeping herself together, and nothing was going to get in her way now.

"To us," Diane said. "Especially you guys who got out of the maze wearing both boots."

Marshall clinked his beer glass against Diane's. "There's no law that says you have to finish with both boots. And you got that dummy out same as the rest of us."

"I believe your time was two seconds shorter than my brother's," Oliver said, elbowing Richard in the ribs.

Tony grinned at his cousin Kevin across the table at the Cape Pursuit Bar and Grill.

He remembered plenty of similar conversations from his own experience and from spending time with new department members. Good-humored teasing went a long way toward building friendships and teamwork, and there were times it was the only way to blow off steam after an ugly call.

"I think Tony lost his helmet once," Kevin said.

"Not in the maze," Tony said, shaking his head. He could feel Laura's eyes on him. Since he was the chief, it was his job to be good at what he did but stay humble. "But I did lose it in the hose race. I think it was the duck and roll that did me in." He laughed. "It's hard to keep your helmet on when you're trying to beat your cousin by diving toward the finish line like you're coming into home plate."

To celebrate the fact that all eight volunteers had passed, the group had agreed to meet for dinner and drinks after they'd all had a chance to go home and shower. No one wore a uniform, not even Tony, Kevin and Gavin. They were off duty and spending time as friends with the department's newest members.

Allen had shown up wearing a T-shirt with the logo of the factory where he worked as a machinist. He hadn't said much, but Tony had seen him smile at least twice. Maybe it was the excellent plates of fried mozzarella sticks, onion rings and potato skins that the waitress had just delivered. Most people around the table were partway through their first drink, but Tony noticed Allen's cup was untouched.

Some of Marshall's cop friends came in and he went over to their table for a few minutes. Tony saw him talking with his hands and laughing, clearly telling a story from his experiences at the state fire academy. His absence at the table left an empty seat next to Laura, and Richard scooted over and sat close to her. Tony felt an instant rush of jealousy. Richard was about Laura's age, single and a decent guy.

But he was also making short work of his second beer and leaning into Laura. She put a finger on his shoulder and gave him a subtle push back into his chair, which he didn't seem to mind. Richard turned and talked to his brother on his other side, also leaning much too close.

Tony let his jealousy go. Richard wasn't being a jerk, but he was a little drunk. His brother appeared to be well on his way to the same condition. Tony pushed his half a beer forward on the table and switched to water, and he noticed his cousin doing the same. They weren't strangers to having a drink together, but Ethan usually came along and drove them. A ten-year veteran of the department, Ethan was the self-appointed and permanent designated driver after growing up with alcoholic parents.

Tony raised a finger and made eye contact with their waiter who came right over. "I think it would be a good idea to get some dinner orders into the kitchen before too many more drinks," he said quietly. The waiter nodded and pulled out a notepad.

He listened to the dinner conversation over the next hour as food came and plates were cleared away. Everyone talked at once, and there was a clear bond among the group at the table. It seemed stronger than usual for volunteer classes. Tony suspected Laura was a reason for that bond, having seen her encouraging everyone. Her study session and insistence on the newspaper article including everyone were also clear evidence that she was in this not for herself alone.

Strangely, she was the quietest person at the table. Serious, even, but not in a sad way. When she had emerged from the maze with the two-hundred-pound dummy in tow, Tony had felt relief greater than he'd ever experienced. He hadn't doubted her ability, but the success rate for the maze for first attempts was far from 100 percent. She wouldn't have been the first one to have to give it another shot, but it would have killed Tony to see her fail.

He wanted to protect her from hardship, failure and anything else that might knock her down. He loved that she was self-assured. As he gazed at her across the table, he realized he loved her.

She raised her eyes to his just as the thought crossed his mind, and Tony was afraid his face betrayed the shocking emotion that rolled through him.

It wasn't just that he wanted to help her save herself—something she didn't appear to need his assistance with—the truth was he loved and cared for her in a way that was nothing like his feelings for his other fellow firefighters.

When everyone had finished eating and the conversation wound down, Tony overheard Laura offering rides home to Richard and Oliver. Marshall had already left because he had an early shift at the police department the next morning. Eighteen-year-old Skip hadn't been drinking, Diane's husband had dropped her off and picked her up, and Brock had stuck with soda all night.

"You okay to drive?" Tony asked Allen.

"Did you see me drinking?" Allen growled. "Just half a one."

"There's your answer."

Tony smiled. "You did a great job today, and you'll be a real asset to the department." He went out on a limb and added, "Your family must be really proud of you."

Allen snorted. "You don't know my family." He cocked his head. "Or maybe you do. My old man got drunk and burned our house down about ten or twelve years ago. Right down to the ground. It was the farmhouse on county road fifteen just south of town."

Tony drew in a slow breath. "I remember that fire. It was one of my first official runs when I joined the department." He vividly remembered the drunk and disorderly home owner, a traumatized wife and kids, and the arson investigation afterward.

"He's out of jail now, but he's still a jerk. On my worst day, I'm better than that."

Tony didn't know what to say, but it made everything he'd observed about Allen make sense. Did Laura know about Allen's family?

"Keys," she was saying to Richard and Oliver.

She held out a hand to each of them, but only Oliver handed over keys. "We drove together. Live just down the street from each other."

"Then it will be easy to drop you off," Laura said.

"I need my car in the morning."

Laura looked over at Tony, her eyebrows raised in a question.

"We can make this work," Tony said.

He loaded Richard and Oliver into his truck, and Laura followed with Richard's car. Luckily, Tony knew the streets of Cape Pursuit well enough to follow the slightly soggy directions from the drunken but cheerful brothers. They had wanted to ride with Laura, but Tony shoved them both toward his truck instead. He glanced in the mirror every ten seconds to make sure Laura was behind him.

After dropping off both brothers and their car, Laura got in Tony's truck for a ride back to the bar.

"That was fun," she said. "What did they talk about on their way home?"

"They compared their performances at the academy today. I have the impression they've been competing for a long time."

"Sibling rivalry," Laura commented.

"You and Nicole don't seem to have a rivalry," Tony said.

He heard her sigh. "No, but we do seem to have a lack of communication this summer." She paused. "No, not communication, just understanding. We both had ways of dealing with Adam's loss. Hers was to throw herself into a different life. New place, new job, new love. It worked for her, and that's great."

"But?"

"But I chose reaching outside myself in a different way." She laughed. "I tried volunteering for everything I could at my high school over the winter, and it helped a little, but this summer I think I've found my true calling."

Tony swallowed. If firefighting was Laura's true calling, he was happy for her, but it left no place for him in her life. A relationship between them, with his being the fire chief, was as impossible as blowing out a house fire as if it were a birthday candle.

"Sadly, it's the worst calling in the world, according to my sister."

"But she's marrying Kevin."

"Kevin isn't her sister. And you remember last summer how long it took her to reconcile herself to the fact that she loved a firefighter."

"So she'll reconcile herself to loving another one," Tony said. "You."

"I hope so."

Tony pulled into the bar's parking lot and

cut the engine, glad when Laura didn't immediately open the door and jump out. It was nice having quiet conversation with her, away from anyone else's ears. If he couldn't give her his love, he could at least offer his friendship.

"What happens next?" he asked.

"I go home and tell my sister about my day whether she wants to hear it or not. I need to share with her what happened to me during the maze."

Tony held his breath, hoping Laura would go on. He suspected something emotional had transpired, but he wasn't in a position to ask.

"I almost gave up at one point," she said, turning to him in the dark pickup. The nearest light in the parking lot sent a shadow over one side of her face.

"It happens to everyone."

"But I kept going. I thought about Adam. I owed it to him to not give up. If he'd had a shred of a chance, even just a sliver of hope, he would have kept going. I couldn't fail. I kept thinking about the power of being able to save someone."

"You did it for him," Tony said quietly, remembering the tears on her cheeks when she pulled off her mask.

"At first, yes. It was as if I could feel him there with me, fighting alongside me. But then, when I got out of the maze and I knew I had done it, it was like starting life all over again."

She brushed her hair behind her ears and leaned forward, and Tony saw her intensity even in the dim light.

"I knew then that my accomplishment was for me, not for Adam. And that's okay. I realized my own power and strength—something I suspected I had but hadn't challenged myself to find. Now that I know it's there for sure, I'm more motivated than ever to be part of the fire department. To save people who need saving, no matter what it takes."

Tony remembered another young firefighter who had been idealistic like that. He'd only been on the department six months when a tragic fire took the lives of three children and there was nothing anyone could do. It had broken his spirit, and he left the service. Tony often wondered what had become of that man, and he never forgot the hollow expression on his face when he turned in his badge.

"That's wonderful," Tony said, knowing that Laura would face terrible things and would have to draw on her strength to handle them. Could she? "I'm really happy for you."

She leaned toward him and touched his shoulder. "I have you to thank for it. You've been a great teacher and mentor."

Her hand lingered on his shoulder for a moment, and then she withdrew and got out of his truck.

Teacher and mentor. Anything more than that would be impossible.

CHAPTER SEVENTEEN

NICOLE'S WEDDING GOWN sparkled in the sun, competing with the glint off the ocean. Laura stood by the trellis and watched her sister and their father walk down an aisle made of beach mats between two groups of white chairs. Laura had arranged for a tent to be on standby, but it wasn't necessary. The mid-July day was pure sunshine and blue sky. Jane stood next to Laura, and across from them, Kevin waited with his brother Tyler and cousin Tony.

It had been a week since Laura had talked with Tony in his truck. She had left so much unsaid, but what choice did she have? Although she had been growing emotionally closer and closer to him all summer, her realization of what she wanted to do with her life had given her a stark choice. Tony or the fire service. She couldn't have both.

She already missed the regular Tuesday

night training sessions. Now that her class had completed their requirements, they were all official volunteers. Laura's cell phone, turned off and in her car for the wedding, was set up to receive notifications when volunteers were needed. She was ready, even anxious, to face her first emergency.

A firetruck, the shiniest pumper, waited in the parking lot closest to the beach wedding, the sun shining off its chrome. At first, Nicole had rejected Kevin's suggestion for a lights and siren ride to the fire station reception after the beach wedding. Laura was glad her sister had changed her mind.

In the front row on the bride's side, Laura's father took a seat next to her mother and watched the wedding begin. Adam should have been there with them. He would have been a groomsman. Would be standing across from Laura with the other firefighters. That was the only missing piece in an otherwise fairytale wedding. Amid the sand, waves and happy faces, there should have been one more smiling member of the bride's family. Laura bit her lip and tried to think about the incredible happiness that was there, not what was missing.

She caught Tony's eye and he smiled at her. In a suit and tie, Tony was irresistibly handsome. But she had to resist him. Now that she had found the occupation that filled her soul, there was no room for Tony—at least there was no room for a man who happened to be the fire chief. There was no way she was going to be a cliché like that. And there was more. Tony had demonstrated over and over that he wanted to protect her. Had treated her specially, watched over her. She had thought he didn't have faith in her, lacked certainty in her ability. But slowly she had realized it was something both better and worse. If he cared for her and wanted to protect her, it would be a distraction. A dangerous one. He had to care equally for all members of the department.

The minister began the ceremony, and Laura held her sister's bouquet so the bride would have her hands free for taking her new husband's hands and exchanging rings. Laura was glad to have something to hold, as it kept her from trembling with emotion. She pushed all thoughts of the fire department from her mind and watched her sister marry the man she loved so much that she was willing to vault over the major obstacles keeping them apart. What must a love like that cost…? Even more importantly, was there a way to estimate its worth?

The photographer snapped pictures, and Laura realized with a shock that those pictures would always be part of her family story now. Their story was evolving in front of her eyes. Tony was in the new pictures along with Tyler and Kevin. Jane had become family. One powerful love had caused the lines around the Wheeler family to blur and evolve. Maybe life was like that, Laura thought. Her own lines around what she believed to be possible had taken on such a new shape she hardly recognized the old boundaries.

The ocean breeze brushed over her neck. She had gone to the salon for a simple updo with Jane and Nicole. Her ocean blue dress left her shoulders and calves bare with a hint of sparkle at the waist. It was surreal, being part of a beach wedding in Cape Pursuit, but it was peaceful. Happy. The audience in white chairs included many members of the community, some family from Indiana and almost all of the Cape Pursuit Fire Department.

The photographer captured Nicole and Kevin's first kiss and Laura felt tears sting her eyes. She fought them back with a huge smile, determined to fill her heart with such joy that there wouldn't be room for anything else. She followed the newlyweds down the aisle and helped her sister onto the back of the fire truck. White lace trailed over the silver steps, and Kevin kept one arm securely around his bride.

Tony got in the driver's seat and leaned out the window.

"Ride shotgun, Laura?"

She shook her head. "I'm driving my parents. See you there."

She would have loved to get in the cab of the truck next to Tony, but she had to choose her family on such an important day. She would have to break the bad news to her parents before they left town, but it would have to wait until after the wedding. She would not ruin her sister's happiness.

The photographer took dozens of pictures of Kevin and Nicole on the truck, and then Tony activated the lights and siren and drove off at parade speed to the fire station. Laura gathered her parents and arranged for her aunts and cousins to follow her. She tucked her bouquet in the back seat and drove her family to the reception where she hoped all her plans would work out.

Her mother leaned forward from the back seat. "It's been wonderful for Nicole to have you here this summer to help make all these wedding plans. I don't know what she would have done without you."

Laura glanced in the rearview mirror and met her mother's smile.

"But we sure will be glad to have you home again," her mother continued.

Laura swallowed and it felt as if an ice cube was sliding down her esophagus. Her sister knew she probably wasn't going back to hall passes and bell schedules, but Laura hadn't dropped the bomb on her parents yet. She was an adult and she could do as she liked with her life. But who would fill the long winter nights for her mom and dad if she chose to stay here? And how was she going to tell them?

She knew one thing for certain—she wasn't telling them on her sister's wedding day. She had also skimmed over the fact that she'd trained for and passed the volunteer exam and was an official member of the department. Instead of telling her parents the truth, she'd given them a vague story about helping out at the fire station in her off hours and allowed them to believe what they wanted. She was playing with fire and taking a risk that no one at the party would tell her parents what she'd been up to. Luckily, they were so focused on Nicole that Laura could fly under the radar. For now.

Laura parked down the street from the fire station where there was also space for her aunt and cousins to park. The trucks were all out of the fire station, staged on the front and rear concrete aprons, ready to go in case of emergency. Laura hoped hard for no emergencies that evening. No fires, no medical issues, no one stepping on something sharp on the beach or pulling a false alarm at a hotel. Nothing that would mar her sister's wedding and send half the guests running for turnout gear.

She'd had a little time to get used to seeing firefighters in suits instead of flame-retardant yellow gear. The ones who attended the beach wedding looked like men she was meeting for the first time. At the station, it was even more surreal to see the dozens of full-time, part-time and volunteer firefighters dressed for a wedding instead of a fire. It was nice.

Her heels clicked on the concrete floor, and Laura almost wanted to laugh at the contrast between her clothing and the life she had chosen that summer. The columns in the station were wrapped in white lights, and banquet tables decorated in blue and silver were scattered around the edges, leaving a sizable dance floor in the middle. Would she dance with the men who had become her colleagues?

"You must be starving," Tony said, appearing right by her side as she walked through the station.

"I'm fine," Laura said, smiling at him. He really was appealing with his cropped blond hair and blue eyes that reflected the colors of the wedding. His eyes and her dress were almost a perfect match.

"You can't be. I've seen you running around all day making sure everything was perfect. You haven't even taken time to have a drink of water or get off your feet."

Protective. Overly so.

"I guess you weren't there in the salon right after brunch when we had our feet up and sipped mimosas while Suzette did our hair," Laura said.

"That was hours ago." Tony lowered his voice and stood close to Laura. At a little over six feet, he was taller than she was but her heels put her at almost eye level. They were behind a column dressed in white lights. It would be so easy to meet his very kissable lips with her own.

And so, so stupid. There wasn't a precedent or a protocol in the big book of firefighting rules about what to do when the chief kissed a member of the department. Laura toyed with the sparkling sash around her waist, looking down where the view of the hard concrete floor was a much safer choice than Tony's sweet mouth and soft blue eyes.

"It was hours ago," she agreed, choosing a playful tone. "So you better not get between me and the buffet line. I'm giving you fair warning."

She turned and walked over to the caterers where she could at least pretend to check on details. The guests flooded in and found tables, and the bride and groom made an entrance. Laura got a plate of food and sat with her parents and relatives from home, even though she was dying to hear the conversation at one of the large tables of firefighters and their wives. One of the older captains was telling stories, and Laura knew from experience they were usually a humorous mixture of fact and fiction.

She belonged in both worlds. The dutiful daughter from Indianapolis, making sure her uncle could find low-salt foods on the buffet table and that her parents were happy. But she also belonged to her new family. As dinner wrapped up and Tyler Ruggles stood to make a speech in honor of his brother, Laura felt her heart trip faster. Her speech was coming up. It was written on an index card in her purse, the medium chosen intentionally to keep it short.

Tyler launched into all the reasons—some of them humorously compelling—why Kevin wasn't good enough for the lovely Nicole but concluded by saying he'd never seen his brother so happy and wishing the new couple well. As Laura stood to give her maid of honor toast, the now-familiar sound of a call from dispatch echoed throughout the station. She froze. Would everyone have to leave? Would she? How would she manage her beautiful satin dress inside turnout gear? The elegant twist Suzette had done her hair in would interfere with the fit of her helmet.

What would her parents say? Oh, sweet goodness…she was going to have to choose between her two families.

Tony held a radio to his ear and pointed to two of the guys who were standing at the back in their uniforms. The three men exchanged a nod, a whole paragraph of silent communication passing between them, and the two on-duty firefighters got in the ambulance behind the station and took off. Because all the doors were open to the warm evening air, everyone at the reception watched them go.

It was just an ambulance run.

"I can hardly compete with that excitement," Laura said, "so I will just say that Nicole and Kevin deserve all the happiness in the world, and they have found it in each other. Their story reminds us all that true love is alive and worth every risk. Congratulations, and I love you." She raised her glass, paused and took a sip of the champagne along with all the guests. Tony's eyes met hers over the rim of his glass, and she looked away because the look she saw in them had nothing to do with putting out fires.

TONY PICKED UP two pieces of wedding cake from the serving table where the remnants of the three-tiered cake sat among a sea of silver forks and blue napkins. He found Laura fussing with a string of white lights at the bottom of a column that had gone out, and he knelt in front of her, offering a piece of cake.

"I don't think anyone's going to notice those lights are out," he said. "There are plenty of others."

"I want it to be perfect," Laura said.

He shrugged. "It is. They have each other and they're leaving on a cruise tomorrow morning. How much better can it get?"

Laura accepted the plate from Tony, but she tipped it as she straightened up and she had to catch the fork in midair before it hit the concrete floor.

"Fast reflexes," he said.

"My nerves are on high alert. I'll probably be too exhausted to run the toaster tomorrow morning."

He had already noticed Laura was organized and good at handling pressure, but he didn't want her to wear herself out. At least not until she'd danced with him, no matter how foolish that might be.

"Let's sit down and eat this cake," he said. "We could talk."

She gave him a questioning glance, but she sat in the chair he pulled out from a table near the edge of the dance floor. The overhead fluorescent lights were turned off, it was dark outside and only the decorative white lights provided a glow.

"Hardly recognize this place," he said. "Unless you close your eyes and take a deep breath."

"I've loved the smell since I walked in here earlier this summer," Laura said. "I think it's tires, engines and old smoke."

"I love it," he said. "But mixed with wedding cake, it's even better."

"Everything's better with cake."

Tony nodded. "Except the groom's dad. With his diabetes, this cake would torpedo his evening."

"Is that why he isn't a firefighter like the rest of the family?"

"Yes. My dad was the lucky brother." Tony glanced over to the table where the older guys sat talking and watching the dancing. "He put in thirty years on the department and retired as chief last summer."

"I saw his picture on the wall. You resemble him, especially the picture of him from when he was younger."

"He's enjoying retirement, but I think he misses it," Tony said. "I sure would."

Laura laughed. "You're pushing thirty, but I think you have a few good years left." She ate a piece of cake and touched the blue napkin to her lips.

Tony wanted to touch his lips to hers and taste their sweetness. He'd known Laura was beautiful from the moment he met her last summer, but her physical beauty had taken on depth this summer and he dreaded the thought of losing her in his life. He couldn't hold her tight and tell her how he felt about her because that would end their friendship. All he could hope for was her time. Being near her.

"What happens at the end of summer?" he asked. Laura put her fork on her empty plate and set it on the table. He saw her look over at the table where her parents and other family members from Indiana sat. "Do your parents know you're not going home?"

She shook her head. "How did you know I'd decided for sure to stay?"

"I've been paying attention," he said, and he hoped she wouldn't ask him to elaborate. He'd paid far too much attention to her.

"I've been putting off telling them, but I'll have to soon." She smiled at him. "I belong here."

He couldn't let himself read too much joy into her simple declaration, and it didn't change things between them. She would be close by but still out of reach.

"Your sister's house will be empty," he said, striving for something practical to talk about. "You could live there. Find a job."

Laura tilted her head as if she were thinking, but she didn't say anything. "Tonight's not the night for mulling over my great transition."

"We could dance instead," Tony said. As soon as he said it, he regretted it. There was a solid chance Laura would reject him, and he'd feel as if he'd wrongly crossed a line and gotten what he deserved. There was a ghost of a chance she'd say yes, and having her in his arms would be the sweetest torture a man could endure. Even worse than fighting an all-day fire in the heat with plenty of water but none to drink.

"Okay," Laura said.

"Unless that would make you uncomfortable," he said, giving her a graceful out if she wanted it.

"Why would it?"

Tony could think of reasons, but he held out his hand instead. The band played a slow song, and there were other firefighters dancing with their wives as well as friends and family on the floor. Everyone danced at weddings. Everyone took someone else's hand and got so close there was nothing between them except the music.

So he shouldn't let it affect him. Shouldn't let her soft fingers in his make him wish the dance would last all night. Shouldn't love how she brushed against him with every move they made together.

"The party will be over in half an hour," she said. "And I'll stay until we get everything cleaned up and put back together."

"I'll stay, too," Tony said.

Even if it wasn't his job as chief to see the station organized and secure, he would have stayed to help Laura, no matter what she was doing.

CHAPTER EIGHTEEN

LAURA SENT HER parents back to their hotel as soon as the bride and groom departed. Her father had eaten too much and his stomach was bothering him, so she insisted they take her car and get some rest. Someone would give her a ride home. She kicked off her high heels and carried them back into the station. It was just before midnight, and there was a lot of work to do. Many of the guests were already gone, but some of the firefighters had stayed to help put the trucks away.

As Laura went around the room and cleared away white tablecloths and centerpieces, Tyler and Gavin followed and folded up the legs on the tables. They stacked them in a corner of the station. Laura nearly crashed into Tony as he strode back and forth, two chairs under each arm, and stacked the chairs near the tables.

"You gave up your heels," he said, pointing to her bare feet.

"I hope there's no rule about wearing shoes in the fire station," she said.

"Not tonight." He smiled and hiked up the chairs under each arm.

Laura finished her task and helped the caterers carry out their serving dishes and utensils. The band members were almost finished hauling out their instruments and sound equipment. She got a stepladder and started unwinding the strings of white lights from the supporting posts that usually served as guides for parking the trucks.

With each minute of effort, the fire station was returning to normal, but Laura would never forget how magical it had been.

"I'll do the high parts," Tony offered, putting a hand on the ladder as Laura stepped down.

"I can handle it," she said.

"But I'm lousy at winding up strings of lights. Christmas is torture. You'd be doing me a favor."

"Okay," Laura agreed. She'd saved the plastic frames the lights came on with the intention of rewinding them all and using them some other time. Maybe a party or Christmas. Where would she be at Christmastime? She'd already thought about taking over the rent on her sister's house now that Nicole would be moving in with Kevin. Of course, she needed to find a full-time job pretty soon. Her teacher's paychecks were spread throughout the year and she still had a few more until they ran out.

"Your parents left with your car," Tony commented as he stood on the ladder, unwound lights and fed them to Laura.

"They were ready to go back to the hotel," Laura said.

"They're not staying with you?"

"No, Nicole's cat is a fur machine and my mom is allergic. It wouldn't be pretty."

"I loved your stories about bringing home stray animals when you were a kid," he commented. "I'm thinking about getting a dog."

"Really? What kind?"

"Whatever kind they have at the shelter that looks lonely," Tony said.

"They all look lonely when you go there, so you have to be really committed to taking only one home."

"I think I'm ready. I used to think my

schedule was too difficult, but now that I'm the chief, I'm in the lucky position of setting my own schedule."

"That's a major perk," Laura commented. "But you have an awful lot of responsibility, too."

"I asked for it." Tony moved the ladder to the next post. "And most of the time I don't mind the added worries."

"Most of the time?" Laura asked as she waited, hands open for the next strand of lights.

"Every so often, I wish I could lay my head on the pillow at night without wondering what might happen before the sun rises."

"You're not alone," Laura said. "Your department is well trained and really great."

Tony nodded. "Which is why I do eventually close my eyes and get some sleep. Most of the time."

They finished taking down the lights, and Tony helped move all the trucks back into their usual parking spots. Laura closed the doors one by one as the trucks came in, and the station became silent and dark. She collected her shoes from the equipment locker with her last name on it.

"Ride home?" Tony asked.

He was both her first and last choice for a ride home. Being with him on and off throughout the day had been hard enough without her heart reaching for him. The dance they'd shared had been a bitter reminder of what she was giving up to dedicate herself to the fire service. In another world, could she have been with Tony as a girlfriend or something more?

"If you can," she said.

"I'm the chief. I can do anything I want," he said with a smile.

"Except sleep at night."

"Right. My truck's alongside the station."

They buckled up and Tony pulled onto the street. "Tired?" he asked.

"Strangely, no. I know it will hit me tomorrow, but I still have party adrenaline in my veins."

Tony cleared his throat. "We could take a walk by the beach."

Laura watched the streetlights of Cape Pursuit pass by. A walk on the beach sounded dangerously close to romantic.

"By the beach," Tony reiterated. "I'd have to take my shoes off to walk in the sand, and

I'm sure not walking barefoot in the dark on that beach."

"Why not?"

"Fish hooks, broken bottles and other creepy stuff. You don't want to step on those, trust me."

Laura laughed. "Your line of work ruins some things for you, doesn't it?"

"Our line of work," he said.

One simple word and she felt included in something important all over again. That feeling of inclusion made Tony's invitation for a walk on the beach seem less dangerous. They were coworkers, even friends. They could unwind together after a big day.

"As long as I don't get my high heels stuck in cracks on the boardwalk, I wouldn't mind stretching my legs and getting some fresh air," she said.

He parked near one of the entrances for the walkway along the beach and they got out. Tony didn't reach for her hand, and Laura considered that a good sign. They were keeping it friendly and professional. If he was being nice to her, maybe it was because he knew he'd have trouble sleeping, too, in his lonely house. Hadn't he said he was thinking of getting a dog?

They began walking and the ocean breeze whipped Laura's dress around her knees. It was cooler than she'd expected, and her bare shoulders and arms felt the chill.

"Take my jacket," Tony said.

"That's okay," Laura protested. It would seem far too much like a date if she accepted his jacket, and she couldn't take that risk.

Tony stopped walking and shrugged out of his suit jacket. He held it out to her. "If you had any idea how tired I was of wearing a suit, you'd know you were helping me out by taking this off my hands."

Laura laughed. "In that case," she said, accepting the suit coat and putting it on, "I'll make a sacrifice."

"You're a team player, Laura Wheeler. I may have to promote you."

"Let me face my first real fire first," she said. "Otherwise people will say it's because we're related."

"We're not related."

"Your cousin married my sister today. That's close enough."

Maybe this was how she could rationalize spending time with Tony and not let her emotions run away with her. They were colleagues and shared common relatives. It wouldn't be strange to have lunch together sometime or go out for pizza. Or take a walk on the beach with his jacket smelling of his scent enveloping her.

Sure, she could handle that.

Tony stopped and turned to her. The walkway was deserted, all the tourists having moved on to bars and hotels for the night. The air was fresh and cool, but Laura felt the warmth of Tony's body clinging to his jacket.

"Laura, I know this isn't right, but—"

She caught her breath and waited. Tony swiped a hand over his eyes and looked up at the stars, rocking back on his heels as he did so.

"Just say it," she said.

He put a hand on her shoulder and stepped closer. "I care about everyone on the department, but my feelings for you are…more."

"They can't be," she said after a long silence. There was so much she wanted to say, but she was afraid to risk the words.

"I can't help it. You're special to me. I

think about you all the time. I've wanted to…"

"Kiss me," Laura said. She wasn't sure if she was finishing his sentence or asking. Tony lowered his face and touched his forehead to hers, giving her the opportunity to say no.

If her feelings for him weren't so strong, she would have backed away. She knew what she was doing when she touched her lips to his, and she didn't stop herself. When their lips met, she was sure she was making the most wonderful mistake of her life.

Tony slid his arms around her and pulled her against his broad chest. He kissed her as if he'd been waiting a long time. She looped her arms around his neck and let herself go… just a little longer.

Finally, and with regret she felt all the way to her bare toes, Laura released her hold on him.

"We can't do this," she said.

"Maybe we could try," he said, taking her hands as she stepped back.

"No. Tony, think about it. You're the fire chief. I'm on your roster. We can't have a relationship. You've already paid too much attention to me this summer."

"No, I haven't. I haven't treated you any differently than anyone else," he protested.

"Yes, you have. At first I thought you didn't think I could handle the physical and emotional challenges."

He held up a hand as if to argue.

"I wasn't mad about it," she said. "You knew about my brother, and you had a right to wonder what I thought I was getting myself into."

"But—"

"But then I realized that instead, you were trying to protect me."

"Of course I want to protect you. I care about you. This is a dangerous job. You—"

"And that's the problem. If you're going to be watching out for me every time we go out on a call, you'll be distracted. It could endanger someone else."

"My men know how to take care of themselves."

Laura shook her head. "I'm not going to be a distraction by having a relationship with you. And I'm not going to be that girl—the one who joins the department and ends up dating the chief. It's…ridiculous."

"Do your feelings for me seem ridiculous?" he asked.

"No," she admitted. "And that's the problem."

"How can you just turn them off like a water valve?"

Laura sighed and tugged her hands away. "You've made sacrifices to be a firefighter. I know you love what you do and would never give it up."

"Everyone makes sacrifices for what they love."

She nodded and swallowed. "That's what I'm doing right now. I can finally get through a day without being blindsided by stabs of grief over my brother. I've found the way to heal my heart and move on by doing something that helps others—the very thing he was trying to do. Now that I've experienced the freedom of being able to take an entire breath without that horrible pain, I can't give it up."

Laura saw the lines of hurt in Tony's face, even in the dim lighting on the boardwalk, but she had to put an end to the attraction between them once and for all.

"I have to choose between you and being a firefighter, even if it breaks my heart."

THE LAST THING Laura wanted the next morning was a confrontation. Was she wrong to choose what was in her heart even if it meant trampling on the feelings of others? Tony hadn't said a word as he'd driven her home after their talk on the beach, and now she was facing two stone-faced parents at the breakfast table.

At least they were outside. The table at the downtown bakery included sunshine and a place for Kevin's dog, Arnold, whom Laura was dog sitting during her sister's honeymoon.

"I'm not doing this to hurt you," Laura said, her coffee and pastry untouched. She hadn't planned to bring the subject up before they ate, but her father had. He'd noticed an equipment locker with the last name Wheeler on it when he'd taken a self-guided tour of the station on his way to the restroom the night before. When he asked Laura about the firefighter named Wheeler, she'd had no choice but to tell her parents it was her locker.

She should have been proud to tell them, but she'd known it wouldn't go over well. Was it cowardice or a desire to shield them from the truth and more pain?

"How can you imagine this wouldn't hurt us?"

"Nicole just *married* a firefighter," Laura said, her tone defensive. She took a calming breath and reached down to pet Arnold as he slept in the shade under her chair.

"That's not the same thing. You know why," her mother said. "I'll be glad when you get home and give up this nonsense."

Laura swallowed. "I'm not coming home. The deadline for resigning my teaching position without penalty is next Monday, and I'm going to call the superintendent and tell him I'm done."

Her parents stared at her, open-mouthed.

"I'm going to stay here in Cape Pursuit, continue volunteering at the station and look for a full-time job," she said, rushing ahead before her parents could ask. The sooner she got it all out in the open, the better. "I may take over the rent on Nicole's house and, as for a job, I've made friends in town and maybe something will come along."

"You're not coming home," her mother said. All anger was gone from her eyes and her voice, and it was replaced by pain.

Laura felt tears welling. She'd hurt her parents who had already suffered the worst thing parents could suffer. And now she was breaking their hearts and leaving them alone. Worse yet, she had found firefighting to be a balm to her own grief, but to her parents it was throwing gasoline on a fire.

"I'm sorry," she said, allowing tears to slip down her cheeks. A truck pulled up in front of the bakery and Tony got out with Travis. They were both in uniform, both carrying radios. When Tony saw Laura in tears at a table with her parents, he stopped dead in his tracks.

"Get a dozen," he said to Travis who politely looked away and went into the bakery without asking questions. "Mr. and Mrs. Wheeler," Tony said, addressing Laura's parents and holding out a hand.

Both her parents sat with their hands in their laps, refusing Tony's friendly gesture.

"You know a fire took our son away,"

Laura's dad said. "And now…" His words became choked and Laura wanted to jump up and hug her father, but she was afraid of falling apart. She had to take her parents to the airport in a few hours, but how could she send them home like this?

"I'm sorry about Adam," Tony said.

Although her heart was breaking, Laura loved the way Tony used her brother's name. It made his condolences personal and it was so much harder than just saying your son. Tony never took the easy way out.

"Laura has joined our department, and she's been through a lot of training. We're glad she's made the decision to be a firefighter."

His tone was soft and kind, and Laura knew Tony was well aware of how much she was sacrificing to join the fire service.

Travis breezed through the door behind him and got in the truck.

"It was nice to meet you, and I hope you have a safe trip home," Tony said, and then he got in the driver's seat of the fire department pickup and pulled away from the curb.

"Come home with us today," her mother said, reaching across the table and putting her hand over Laura's. "It will clear your head and give you time to think."

"I can't," Laura said. "I have to go back to work tomorrow. I traded my day off to have yesterday free."

"So you're just…staying," her father said.

"I promise you I've thought a lot about this. I know it won't make sense to you that becoming a rescuer has actually saved me from my own grief."

"We can't take any more heartbreak," her father said.

Her parents stared at her with sad eyes.

The trip to the airport a few hours later was as silent as an empty house. There were volumes of things Laura knew her parents wanted to say, and she would have loved to have been able to put her feelings into words, but they were at a place where they couldn't meet.

Not yet, anyway.

Laura went straight to a secluded section of the beach when she returned from the airport so she could watch the waves and think. She sat in the sand and thought about the ground she had gained that summer, but also the losses she'd caused.

Nicole had come around, slowly. If she weren't on a cruise ship somewhere, maybe Laura could have talked with her about their parents. But Nicole deserved her happiness.

And what about Tony? He would understand. He'd seen what was going on when he stopped by their table. She'd hurt him the night before, she'd thrown her parents back into misery after the happy wedding and now what? As Laura sat on the sand, she scooped it up and let it fall in cascades back onto the beach.

She could give up the fire service. Maybe her own happiness wasn't worth destroying the happiness of others. Her parents would be overjoyed if she came home and continued just as they had been. And Tony? If she gave up the fire service, she could date him without guilt, but that would lead to other pain and her giving up would always come between them.

Laura lay back on the sand and let the sun bake her eyelids. It would be so easy just to say her summer had been a whim and she was quitting the station and leaving Cape Pursuit. Back home, no one would even know.

Except her. She would know how she'd clawed open the cage of her grief and escaped just to turn around and thrust herself back in.

She sat up. She had not come this far just to give up. Laura dug her phone out of her back pocket. Her parents would be on the plane by now, but she could leave them a voice mail telling them how much she loved them even though she knew they disapproved of her choices. As she left the message, her phone buzzed. She checked the screen when she disconnected and saw something that stopped and then kick-started her heart.

Her phone displayed a wide red bar, an alert notification calling volunteers to the station for a fire.

CHAPTER NINETEEN

IF HE'D KNOWN how much danger the neighboring house was in, Tony would have called in the volunteers much sooner. Kitchen fire. That was what the dispatcher said. Maybe the fire started in the kitchen, but when he rounded the corner of the residential street, smoke was rolling out the front door in dark gray plumes.

It was a seething, working house fire on a street with houses packed tight together. A car was parked in front of the hydrant across the street, violating the law and making a bad situation worse. Gavin hopped down and hooked the hydrant while Tony parked the pumper in the middle of the street that he was officially closing.

He radioed the station and ordered the ladder truck, rescue truck, backup pumper and tanker. Basically, everything. The volunteers who were available on a Sunday afternoon were going to make the difference between losing the neighboring houses or not.

He tried very hard not to think about Laura being one of those volunteers. She'd mentioned driving her parents to the airport that afternoon. Maybe she would still be out of town, safe from the flames no matter how much she would regret missing her first big fire. He knew she was right...that his desire to protect her was a distraction and a potential danger.

A man came out from the house across the street with car keys in his hand. Tony was in no mood for niceties.

"If that's your car," he said, "you have five seconds to move it."

He felt anger rolling off him in waves. Their job was going to be hard enough without bystanders being stupid. The man jumped into his car.

With the hydrant now cleared, Gavin had a hose hooked up and waiting.

"Anyone in there?" Tony asked the people assembled on the lawn. A woman shook her head. "We're renting it for the week. My husband is at the beach with the kids and I was starting dinner. I don't know what happened."

"We live next door," another man said. He pointed to his house, which was only about fifteen feet from the fire.

More trucks arrived with full-timers and volunteers, and two firefighters suited up with air packs went in the front door with a hose. Tony stayed outside, running the pump on the truck and keeping an eye on the entire scene. The backup pumper arrived, and his heart sank when he saw Laura jump off the back.

"Need to send two more in through the garage entrance and drive the flames out through the kitchen," Tyler said.

Tony nodded. "Suit up."

Laura, Allen and Ethan came up to Tony.

"Tyler's going in through the garage, you go with him and keep a hand on the hose," he told Allen.

"I can—" Laura began.

"Need a water curtain between the houses," Tony said. He pointed to Laura and Ethan. "You two set it up and babysit it."

Laura turned and followed Ethan without a word. What he was asking her to do was important, maybe even more than going inside with a hose. This house was well on its way to being a total loss, but the one next door could be saved. Tony watched anxiously, keeping an ear on the radio for communication from his four men inside. The flames rolling out the door slowed and he heard Gavin on the radio saying they'd knocked down the fire.

Ethan and Laura had two hoses trained on the side of the burning house and the space between it and the next home. They alternately hosed down the roof and siding of the house next door, making an effective shield against that one going up in flames, too. It was a textbook way to fight and contain a fire, and the danger was over within thirty minutes.

What wasn't textbook was the anxiety Tony felt seeing Laura before the burning house. She was doing exactly what she was supposed to do, but Tony couldn't help wanting to go to her and shield her from the heat and smoke. What if the wall fell or part of the roof collapsed? She could be in danger. Would Ethan act fast enough to save her?

They loaded up wet, dirty equipment and

returned to the station several hours later, after going through the house looking for hot spots, securing the wreckage and writing a report.

"Could've been worse," Gavin commented as he drove the pumper. Tony rolled the window down and propped his elbow on the door frame. "I thought the house next door might be a goner when we first rolled up."

"Good water curtain," Tony commented. Good, but he couldn't stop thinking about the snap decision he'd made to send Allen into the fire and Laura to protect the house next door. If she had been one of the guys, would he have sent her in as he had Allen? She had exactly the same training and experience.

In his heart, he knew the answer, but what mattered was what was in Laura's heart.

She had arrived at the station a few minutes before Tony and was already scrubbing hose on the concrete apron. She had her helmet and coat off but wore her bunker pants and boots as she used a long-handled brush to remove soot from the white hose. He remembered seeing her in a green T-shirt that morning as she sat with her parents outside the bakery, none of them touching their pastries and coffee.

What a day.

Of the new class of volunteers, only Laura, Allen, Brock and Diane had shown up. Diane was too late to get on a truck, so she'd stayed in the radio room. Brock had helped direct traffic around the block and away from the scene, and Laura and Allen had gotten direct roles in fighting the fire.

"Nice job," Tony heard Travis telling Allen and Laura as they worked together to clean hose. "Your first big fire."

"That wasn't a big fire," Gavin said, waving his hand as if he were shooing away a bird. "Hardly got your feet wet," he added, smiling.

"Wet enough," Travis said. "You did a good job staying right on my tail and keeping hold of the hose, Allen. Most important thing, never let that hose go or you could be toast."

Tony watched Laura's face as Travis spoke. He knew she would have done just as well if he'd given her the chance.

"Hey," Ethan said, giving Laura a friendly

one-armed hug. "I believe we were the ones who saved the neighbor's roof."

"And siding," Laura added. "Although I don't think that hibiscus plant is going to bloom again this year."

"There was a plant?"

Laura nodded. "You were standing in it."

"Then it didn't burn," Ethan said. "That's a win."

When the hoses were in the dryer, the trucks washed and the extra firefighters gone home, Tony saw Laura laying her gloves on top of her locker so they would dry better. Now or never.

"Hi," he said, leaning one shoulder against the post by her locker. She acknowledged him with half a smile. "How did it go with your parents?"

"Do you ask all the firefighters about breakfast with their parents?" she asked, reminding him painfully of her first visit to the fire station.

Tony's shoulders fell. "I'm sorry."

Laura pushed her boots into the space at the bottom of the locker. "Don't be. It's not your fault that it was pretty bad, and I think it's going to be a while before they forgive me."

"They should have seen you in action this afternoon."

"In action hosing down the neighbor's house instead of going in?"

"Not everyone goes in," Tony said, defending himself.

Laura crossed her arms. "You had two equal choices in me and Allen. As equal as you can get except for one thing."

"If this is about you being a woman—"

Laura turned and walked out of the station. Tony followed, walking quickly to catch up to her. She whipped around when she heard him behind her.

"*Is* it because I'm a woman?"

Tony searched his mind for the right answer, but he didn't know what it was. So he went with the truth. "No. It's because you're you."

"Me?"

Tony put his hands over his face, not caring if he was leaving dirt streaks, wishing he could go back and do a lot of things differently. But when he focused on Laura standing in front of him, her cheeks flushed and shoulders back in defiance, he knew there was nothing he could have changed.

"It's because you're you," he repeated. "And I love you."

He saw her swallow as she stared at him with shock. The seconds dragged past. Finally, she held up one finger.

"No," she said. "Don't you dare. This is why I said we could not have a relationship. It would ruin everything I've worked for. Do you know what happened today after the fire was out? Even though I thought I'd drawn a less important job, it meant the world to the people who lived next door. The family who lived there actually came up and gave me a hug and said thank you for saving their house. I helped save their house. They'll never forget it, and neither will I. It's exactly why I wanted to be where I am."

"You did a great job," he said. "I knew you would."

Laura shook her head. "You're a good teacher, Tony. But there's one thing you never told us in class, and that was how good it would feel to do something important for someone else."

"I couldn't."

"I know. It's something we have to find out for ourselves. Earlier today, I almost considered calling it quits with the fire service. I questioned whether I had the right to break my family's hearts for my own happiness and satisfaction."

"I'm glad you didn't," Tony ventured, afraid to say much more.

"I am, too. I'm not letting them stand in my way no matter how much I love them. And I'm not letting you make me question what I'm doing here, either."

He noticed she did not add, *No matter how much I love you.*

"If you say you love me, there's only one way you can prove it to me and that's by letting me do my job and trusting me to do what's right for myself."

Laura left without giving him a chance to respond, which was just as well. Tony couldn't think of a single word that would make things better.

"COMES IN THREES," Kevin commented on the way home from the airport. Nicole told her sister all about their cruise for the first thirty minutes of the drive, and then Kevin wanted to know what had been going on at the station during their week's honeymoon. Laura told him about the house fire the day after the wedding and another house fire caused by faulty wiring. That one the volunteers had also been called out on, but Laura had been the only person working the beach shack and couldn't leave.

She'd gone to the station an hour later when she got off work, but the situation was under control so she stuck around and helped clean up.

"Don't say that," Nicole said. "Just because there were two house fires this week doesn't mean there's going to be another."

"Just saying," Kevin said. "It seems to happen."

"We should have gone on a longer cruise," Nicole said. "I talked to Mom when we got back into port."

"Is she still mad?" Laura asked. The previous Sunday had been one of the most painful and yet exhilarating days of her life. The hug from the family whose house she'd helped save had made everything else worthwhile. Even her parents' disappointment in her, even Tony's crushed expression when she all but told him to get out of her way.

She had seen his face every time she closed her eyes this week. Why did she have to fall in love with the one man she couldn't have?

"Still mad, but the message you left them went a long way. They may come around sooner than I will," Nicole said.

"Hey," Laura said, laughing. "I thought you were on my side already. Remember the top layer of your wedding cake is in my freezer, and if you make me sad enough, I might just eat it."

"You wouldn't," Nicole said.

"Probably not, but you should be nice to me just in case."

Laura took the newlyweds home where Arnold was already waiting. The old dog made a big effort to get up and wag his tail, even putting his paws on Kevin's knees as a welcome. Laura had also brought Nicole's cat, Claudette, over earlier in the day, but the cat was hiding under a bed as a silent protest to her new dwelling. Laura hoped she'd come around.

The sun was setting as Laura pulled into

her driveway. Over the past week, she'd gotten used to the idea of having her sister's house all to herself, but seeing her sister glowing with happiness over her marriage made Laura's empty house seem lonelier.

Maybe she should get a dog. She wondered if Tony had gone to the shelter to find a companion. A man as sweet and decent as Tony deserved to be happy. She sighed. He had offered her his affection, and she'd pushed him away with both hands. Did he understand?

Laura would like to have talked with her sister about Tony, but she couldn't do that with Kevin in the car, too. Besides, her sister deserved to have her honeymoon last, without being interrupted by someone else's drama.

Laura put her purse and phone on the kitchen table and dug through the freezer for something she could microwave and eat on the back deck. She pulled out a plastic container that looked as if it might contain leftover pot roast.

Her phone vibrated on the table and Laura leaned over to look at it. A red alert band. She shut the freezer door, grabbed her keys and took off without even reading the description. Whatever it was, she was going to the fire department to do what she could.

As she drove to the station, she tried to stay within speed limits and obey every stop sign to the letter, but her adrenaline fought her all the way. When she finally turned onto the fire station's street, she parked, ran inside and suited up.

She didn't have to ask if it was a fire because all the men were getting into their yellow turnout gear and two of the fire trucks were already running, filling the station with the soft rumble of their power.

"Pumper one," Tony yelled, pointing at Laura and Charlie. "Put your tanks on en route."

Tony drove, Ethan rode shotgun and Laura and Charlie got in the back. "What do we know?" Laura asked.

"Two-story house, neighbor called it in, fire has a huge start," Charlie said. He and Laura put their arms through the straps on their air packs set up so a firefighter could easily slide into the pack on the way to a fire. Laura had practiced the maneuver many times both with her group and when she thought no one was looking. It was difficult with the heavy coat, but she did it.

"Do we know if the fire is on the first or second floor?" she asked. She was running scenarios through her head on how they could attack the fire, even though she knew Tony would make those decisions. Would they set up the ladder truck? Get on the roof and ventilate the fire? Go inside and attack it? Most importantly, was Tony really going to send her in? He'd had a chance once before and didn't. She'd called him on it, but had she really changed his mind?

And what would it mean if she had?

"Probably both floors by the time we get there. Fire moves fast," Charlie said. "I hate it when a neighbor calls it in because you never know if the occupants are home and trapped or just lucky enough to not be home."

"How will we know if there's anyone trapped?"

"We won't," he said. "Not until we look. Which makes our jobs a whole lot tougher. We'll send in two teams right away. One to search for victims, one to knock down the fire. If we're the search team, remember victims are usually hiding under something."

Laura thought of her brother, his body found under the fire blankets that were supposed to save him and his crew from the rapidly advancing forest fire. She pushed that thought away and reviewed everything she knew about search and rescue on the drive to the fire.

"We'll pull up, Ethan will hook a hydrant, we'll get a charged line. Be ready, and whatever you do, breathe slowly. You may have to conserve your air and energy so you can save my butt," Charlie said, grinning.

When the truck stopped, everything happened so fast Laura thought about that one thing: breathing slowly. She took hold of a charged line, and Tony turned on her tank as he yelled, "Neighbors don't know if anyone's home, but there's a car in the driveway." He tapped her helmet. "Go."

Tony was sending her into the fire. It was her chance to save someone as Adam could not be saved. A direct chance to right the past. And it was the one thing Tony could do to prove he loved her. Was that why he chose her to pair up with Charlie and put on the air packs?

What mattered now was her training, her partner and the chance that her actions could mean the difference between life or death for another human being. She followed Charlie and they did a quick sweep of the downstairs. Crouching low under the smoke, their visibility was poor, but they didn't see anyone in the kitchen, living room, dining room or bathroom. Charlie tapped her shoulder and pointed up.

Bedrooms. There weren't any on the first floor, but given the size of the home there could be at least three bedrooms upstairs. It was evening, too early for bedtime, so she hoped the bedrooms would be empty. She followed Charlie up the stairs, taking her share of the weight of the hose. Framed photos hung along the wall on the way up the staircase, but Laura couldn't make out the pictures through the smoke. A pair of firefighters behind them on the first floor was already knocking down the flames they found downstairs. Laura couldn't tell who they were, but she knew her mission wasn't to put out flames. She and Charlie had been sent in to find any entrapped victims.

They were on the landing when Laura heard radio traffic from the mic on her shoulder. She tried to listen. Was the voice saying no entrapped victims? Charlie motioned in front of him, indicating they were going on. Maybe Laura hadn't heard correctly. On their knees, Charlie and Laura pushed open a bedroom door and looked inside. It was a nursery with a crib under the window. They moved fast across the room and looked into the crib. Empty. She saw Charlie shake his head and point toward the door, and then she heard Tony's voice on the radio, distinctly this time, saying the home was unoccupied according to a neighbor who saw a car leave earlier.

Charlie must have heard the same thing because he moved toward the door and turned back toward the staircase, ignoring the other rooms on the second floor. Laura started to follow him, and then she saw something that changed her mind.

A diaper bag. On the floor next to the crib. She stared at it for a moment, trying to match thoughts up in her head. Doesn't a mom always haul the diaper bag with her if she's taking the baby somewhere? She'd helped Jane lug hers around, and she'd done plenty of babysitting as a teenager.

If the bag was still there...

Laura tugged at Charlie's coat, and when he turned around she pointed to the bag on the floor. The smoke and his mask obscured his features, but his next action told her he understood what she was saying. He entered the room and swept it, looking in the closet first. He started to move rapidly and Laura kept up. They continued down the upstairs hall that they had nearly abandoned.

The next room was a bathroom. Laura was first through the door and right in front of her was a woman sitting on the floor by the bathtub holding a wet towel over a baby's face. The woman's knees were up to her chest and she huddled against the tub as if she thought there was no hope. When she saw Laura and Charlie, Laura thought her own heart would explode at the look of absolute relief on the mother's face. Laura held out her hands for the baby out of instinct. It was a girl, dressed in a pink sleeper. She had dark hair, but her face was red from crying.

Laura soaked a towel with the bathtub faucet and wrapped the baby. She opened the front of her coat and tucked the baby inside. She heard Charlie asking the mother if anyone else was home and saw her shake her head. Charlie said something over the radio, and he picked up the mother and carried her out of the bathroom. Laura was right behind him, the baby clutched inside her coat.

There was no time to be careful, no time to care about keeping track of the hose or anything else. She was racing the clock and the flames to get the baby down the stairs and through the front door.

Two firefighters waited at the bottom of the stairs, a hose in hand, but Charlie hurried past them and Laura followed, sheltering the baby inside her coat and turning her back to the heat and smoke. They burst through the front doors and Laura breathed again. She dropped to her knees on the front lawn and opened her coat.

Charlie lowered the mother to the ground in the grass, and two more firefighters came over with oxygen and a stretcher. A firefighter held out his hands for the baby, and Laura carefully gave the shrieking infant to him. As she laid the baby in his hands, she looked up and saw Tony's face. He looked dumbfounded, as if she had just produced a miracle from the front of her coat.

Laura heard a bell ringing and remembered the sound from their training. It indicated low air in a breathing tank. Tony handed the baby to Tyler, and then he reached up and disconnected Laura's air hose. He loosened the strap on her helmet and helped her ease it off along with her mask.

"Are you okay?" he asked.

"Are the mother and baby okay?"

He glanced over. "They're both crying, and that's not a bad sign. Where did you find them? The neighbor said he saw a car leave an hour ago, but obviously the whole family wasn't in it."

"Bathroom. We were going to give up searching when you radioed, but then I saw the diaper bag. Made me think the baby was somewhere in the house."

Tony smiled. "Can't leave home without that."

Laura sat back on her heels and shivered. Now that the adrenaline surge had rushed through her and she was away from the heat, she felt gooseflesh all over her body. Everything had happened so quickly, and the downstairs was still burning. She knew two firefighters were inside, and there were at least six more all around the fire scene, manning the pump, setting up a ladder and taking care of the victims she and Charlie had pulled from the fire.

Tony stood up and spoke into his radio. It was an active fire scene, and he was in charge, responsible for everyone. Laura got to her feet and went over to the ambulance where the mother and baby were tucked inside.

"Okay?" Laura asked.

"Are you the one who carried—" the mother asked. She couldn't even articulate the words through her tears, but Laura knew what she was asking. She nodded. "What's her name?"

The mother almost smiled. "Melanie."

Laura stepped into the ambulance and took a quick look at the little girl, who appeared to be only a few months old. So young, and already a survivor.

"Going with us?" Tyler asked.

Laura shook her head. "No. You go." She

shot the mother an encouraging smile and backed quickly out of the ambulance. It sped away, lights flashing and sirens blaring. Nicole rushed down the street and barreled into Laura, hugging her so tight Laura realized she had seriously underestimated her sister's strength.

"That wasn't you in there," she said. "Or Kevin?"

"No. It was a mother and baby who were trapped in the fire."

Nicole clapped a hand over her mouth. "Oh, my God. Are they—?"

"They're okay," Laura said. "We saved them."

"We?"

"Me and Charlie. I got to carry the baby out."

Nicole put her arms around her. "My sister the hero. I'm so proud of you. But you need a shower. Come home with me."

"Not yet," Laura said. "We're not done yet."

A car careened down the street and a man got out and ran flat out at Olympic speed for the front door of the house without paying attention to everyone who was shouting at him to stop. Tony stepped in his way and held his ground. The man crashed into him and they both fell back against the front wall of the house. Tony picked the man up and held him at arm's length. Laura watched, flabbergasted, as Tony turned the man around and physically marched him over to Laura and Nicole.

"Tell him his wife and baby are okay," Tony said.

Laura briefly explained what had happened, leaving out the scary details.

"I'm going to the hospital right now," he said, his eyes wild and his breath ragged.

Nicole stopped him. "I'll drive you," she said.

"I don't even know you," the man said.

"My husband is a firefighter," she said, pointing out Kevin who was on a ladder over the porch roof. "More importantly, my sister is the one who saved your wife and baby. I think you can trust me."

Hearing the pride and approval in Nicole's voice made Laura believe without a doubt that she had found where she belonged. She picked up her fire helmet and put it back on. Gavin was getting a tall ladder off the side of one of the pumpers and Laura went over to help him lift it down and carry it. It felt good to be doing something useful, and their work was far from over. She held the bottom of the ladder as Gavin climbed it and fed him hose to put through a second story window.

Later, after the fire was out, she helped load equipment back on the trucks to be cleaned and inspected back at the station. Tony came over and stood next to her in the dark shadows of the truck.

"I keep wondering what would have happened if I'd sent someone else in to search for victims," he said, his voice soft and serious. "Would someone else have noticed that one little detail that ended up saving two lives?"

Laura swallowed the lump in her throat. She did not want to have this conversation with Tony now. No one could see them where they were on the back side of a fire truck in the dark. Many of the trucks had already left, and the floodlights were being turned off one by one as the scene wound down.

"Everyone is well trained and incredibly dedicated," she said. "I think anyone would have done what I did."

Tony shook his head, his fire helmet exaggerating the movement. "We'll never know, but I do know it's a damn good thing you let me have it after the last fire, or I might not have chosen you to go in. That decision might have meant…"

Laura put both hands on Tony's shoulders. "Everything turned out fine," she said.

Tony took one of her hands, held it for a moment in his and then kissed the back of her hand.

"Almost," he said.

CHAPTER TWENTY

"You're in the paper," Nicole said when she came over the next afternoon. "You've got to see this picture."

Laura had just gotten home from her job at the beach and she wanted to shower off the sunscreen and sand. She loved the beach, but each passing day reminded her that she really needed to get a grown-up job if she was planning to stay in Cape Pursuit.

"I'm glad you're here," Laura said. "I have a plan to run past you, and I know you well enough to know that you'll be brutally honest with me if you hate it."

"Aren't you going to look at the article?" Nicole said. She got two cans of soda out of the fridge and opened the kitchen door to the back porch.

"Fine," Laura said. She sat in one of the chairs on the back deck and opened the newspaper. "Okay," she said. "Wow. I guess

I see what you're talking about, but I don't even remember anyone taking this picture."

"You were busy saving babies," Nicole said.

"Just one."

The picture was of the moment Laura had knelt on the ground outside the burning house and opened the front of her coat to reveal a baby wrapped in a towel. The caption below gave Laura's name and stated she was a new member of the department.

"Poor baby Melanie," Laura said. "I hope she doesn't remember any of this."

"She won't. But her family will never forget it."

The sisters were silent for a few minutes as they watched the bird feeder and drank their soda on the quiet late afternoon day.

"Adam would be proud," Nicole said.

Laura fought tears. Despite the incredible emotion of the night before and the chatter about her heroism all day long at work, she had kept her feelings in check and tried not to think about what could have happened. What did happen to someone her family loved very much.

"Don't make me cry," Laura said.

Nicole sat back in her chair and put her feet up on the deck railing. "I talked to Mom and Dad today," she said. Laura felt her heart sink. "I told them what happened last night. They got online and saw the picture and article on the newspaper website while we were still on the phone together. Of course there was a lot of swearing because dad has a new laptop and he says he can't get used to it, but I eventually got them to the front-page story in the *Cape Pursuit News*."

"What did they say?"

"They said you were a hero, they accepted your decision to be a firefighter and they wanted grandchildren," Nicole said.

"What?"

"That last part was for me since I've been married a week and a half now, but I think the picture of the baby inspired it."

Laura wanted to laugh, but she knew there would never be a better time to tell her sister what had been on her mind for two long years. "It's my fault Adam is dead."

Nicole's mouth opened in shock for a moment and then she shook her head. "No, it isn't."

"I was the one who told him about that

summer job. I was helping him with his final paper at the end of the semester. I sent him a picture of the flyer I'd seen downtown advertising the summer firefighting job."

Laura waited for her sister's anger, but it didn't come.

"I know," Nicole said. "Adam told me. And Mom and Dad."

"He did?" Laura couldn't believe that what she had considered her secret guilt was no secret, and her family had never said a word of blame to her.

Nicole nodded. "I assumed you knew that. And it doesn't make you any more responsible than the rest of us. None of us tried to stop him."

A heavy slice of guilt fell away from Laura, even though the pain of losing her brother would always be part of her.

"Is that partly why you've...struggled so much?" Nicole asked. "And maybe why being a firefighter is so important to you now?"

"Part. But not all. I really love knowing I can help someone and whenever I do, I think of Adam and wish there had been someone to rescue him."

"Me, too," Nicole said. "But I'm glad you're out there doing what you can."

Laura sipped her soda for a moment and decided it was time. "So, if I enrolled in a professional firefighting course and decided to make it my full-time job, I would have my family's full support?"

Nicole grinned. "You're totally taking advantage of good timing, but yes, you would."

"I'm going to," Laura said. "I'd been thinking about it, but I needed to be tested first, needed to prove myself."

"To who?"

"To me," Laura admitted. "And I passed the test."

"Heck, yes, you did," Nicole said, clinking her can against her sister's. "Have you told Tony yet?"

"No. I'll ask him for a letter of recommendation when I get the application for fire school."

"Is that really how you're going to handle this?" Nicole asked. "Don't think I haven't noticed how you feel about him."

Laura shrugged, knowing there was no point her denying her sister's intuition. "I don't have any better ideas." She'd tried to read into his behavior at the fire scene. He'd treated her just like any other firefighter on the way to the scene, had sent her in without—to her knowledge—a second thought. But she highly doubted he kissed the hands of any of the other firefighters when the fire was over. She sure hoped not.

She'd challenged him to prove his love by letting her do what she needed to do. And he'd done exactly that. Did that mean he loved her or that he was letting her go?

"I have a better idea," her sister said. "Everyone in the county thinks you're the bravest person alive, so you should go prove it."

"How?"

"By telling him that you love him," Nicole said. "I'd fake a 911 call to get him over here, but it wouldn't look very good if the wife and sister of a firefighter did that."

"I'll handle this," Laura said. "If only to keep you out of trouble."

TONY HAD JUST finished the fire reports from the night before and hit Save on the desktop in his office when his cell phone pinged. *Laura.* He'd been thinking about her all night and all day. He was well aware he could have been filling out a double fatality report instead of the far better news of the total loss of a home but no loss of life. Laura's instinct and quick thinking had made all the difference. She had to be happy. But did that happiness include him?

The message on his phone had only one word. Boardwalk?

She didn't need to explain any further. He vividly remembered their walk the night of the wedding and how sadly it had ended. He'd told her he cared, and she'd told him he wasn't allowed to.

That hadn't stopped him.

Did she want to reopen that conversation or simply reiterate what she'd said before? Had last night's fire changed things between them for better or for worse? He had to know.

Five minutes?

Okay.

Tony closed his office door, popped his head into the bunk room where three on-duty guys were watching the evening news and said, "I'm taking off for the night."

He got in his truck and drove to the beach boardwalk, thoughts of Laura swirling through his mind. Was he foolish for getting his hopes up? When he parked his truck, he hardly remembered taking the keys out of the ignition. He took two steps away, then went back to deposit his phone and radio on the seat. He was off duty, for once.

She was already there on the boardwalk, standing with her face turned to the ocean. She wore a loose white blouse that floated in the breeze and made her look like one of the many carefree tourists enjoying a summer's day.

Laura turned and saw him, and her smile gave him a shot of encouragement. He made himself take long, slow steps instead of running. He wanted to scoop her into his arms, but he settled for standing only inches from her, one hand on the railing. They faced each other in silence for a moment.

"The whole town is talking about you," he said, breaking the tension.

"I hope they're talking about Charlie, too. He carried a woman out of a burning house."

Tony laughed. "Who cares about Charlie? You pulled a baby out of your turnout coat.

That's solid gold in the realm of public opinion. And in my opinion."

Laura smiled. "That's not what I asked you here to talk about."

"Good."

"This has been quite a summer. When I got here, I didn't want to go back to my old life, but I didn't know what I wanted to do instead. That beach rescue my first week…" she paused and raised her eyes to meet his "…it led me straight to you."

"I'm glad," he said, resisting the urge to wrap his fingers over hers on the railing.

"I felt empowered again for the first time since Adam died. It was as if there was something I could do to move forward without always being hindered by that awful, senseless loss. The more I trained and learned, the stronger I felt."

Tony listened with every nerve in his body, hoping the conversation was going where he wanted it to, needed it to.

"But there was something in my path. Someone, actually," she said. "I refused to let my feelings for you get in my way."

"Sorry," Tony said.

"Don't be. It wasn't your fault I fell in love with you a little more every single day."

"You did?" he said, hope taking flame inside him.

"But that was the problem. I couldn't be with you and also be on the department, especially when you were acting like a big protective mama bear."

"Let's go with papa bear if you ever tell this story to anyone else."

Laura laughed. "And I was also afraid of confusing my feelings about firefighting with my feelings for you."

"And now?" he asked, taking her hand.

"Now I'm sure I love firefighting."

"And?" Tony asked, feeling almost certain he knew where she was going.

"And I love you."

Tony wrapped his arms around her and kissed her forehead.

"Not so fast," she said, but she didn't move away. Instead she looped her arms around his neck. "You haven't heard my plan for staying in Cape Pursuit."

"Fine," he said. "I'll demote myself and make you chief. I think everyone likes you better anyway, and you definitely have better press coverage."

Laura laughed. "You don't have to go that far. I've decided to enroll in fire school and become a professional firefighter."

Tony held her close and took a deep breath of ocean air. "I'm not surprised, and I would never stand in your way. You can't teach someone instinct and passion, and you have both."

"I can't promise I'll work on the Cape Pursuit Department when I finish my classes," she said. "There are other departments close by, though, so I hope I could stay in town."

"I respect that," he said, "but I may try to change your mind because I want to recruit the best firefighters for my crew."

Laura kissed him, long and sweet as her fingers played through his hair. Tony never wanted to leave that boardwalk if he could keep her in his arms.

"I love you," she said.

"And I love you."

"There's just one thing more that I need," Laura said.

"Anything."

"I need an excellent study partner for my classes."

"I'm your man," Tony said, holding her close and feeling a greater happiness than he'd ever known.

* * * * *

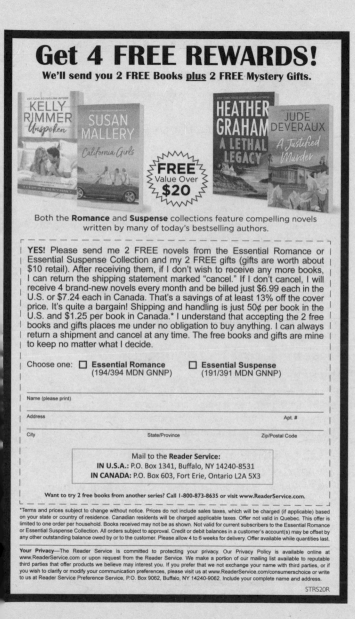

ReaderService.com has a new look!

We have refreshed our website and we want to share our new look with you. Head over to ReaderService.com and check it out!

On ReaderService.com, you can:

- Try 2 free books from any series
- Access risk-free special offers
- View your account history & manage payments
- Browse the latest Bonus Bucks catalog

Don't miss out!

If you want to stay up-to-date on the latest at the Reader Service and enjoy more Harlequin content, make sure you've signed up for our monthly News & Notes email newsletter. Sign up online at ReaderService.com.